I, Sherlock Holmes

Untold Adventures
of
Sherlock Holmes

I, Sherlock Holmes

Untold Adventures of Sherlock Holmes

Written and Illustrated
by
Dr. Vincent J. Francavilla

NFB Publishing
119 Dorchester Road
Buffalo, New York 14213
For more information visit Nfbpublishing.com

Dedicated with Love
to My Wife, Susan,
with Gratitude
to My Brother, Joseph

To Janice for her creative contributions.

The Stories

List of Illustrations:

ADVENTURE No. 1

I, Sherlock Holmes

I, SHERLOCK HOLMES

It was raining. Nature seemed to be in deepest mourning at the loss of one of its most lovely creations.

I had lost my older sister, Violet-Rose. The sister who had calmed my fears when I was a little child, walked with me when I was lonely, and held my hand when I needed a friend. She was more than a mother. For my mother, and indeed both of my parents, simply could not take the time to understand me; father, with his many duties for the British government, and mother, with her many social causes and now not with the family anymore. But my sister, Violet-Rose, had always been able to talk to me, giving encouragement when life presented me with my greatest challenges. There would never be another woman to teach my soul how to laugh.

I can still hear her words to me.

"Sherlock, you must live life … taste all of its flavors to the fullest. Time is short … you never know when the Lord calls."

How prophetic! My sister was a young woman in the flowering of her youth. She was so full of fun and promise. Her gifts for music and poetry were astounding. I cannot forget the last poem she ever wrote.

"How like a flame is life
Filled with the spark and brilliance of youth
Probing the darkness in search of truth
Too soon extinguished...that flame of life.
How brilliantly does the torch burn
Reaching for that unattainable goal
Looking to heaven to heal one's soul
No more does that torch burn!"
        ...for James

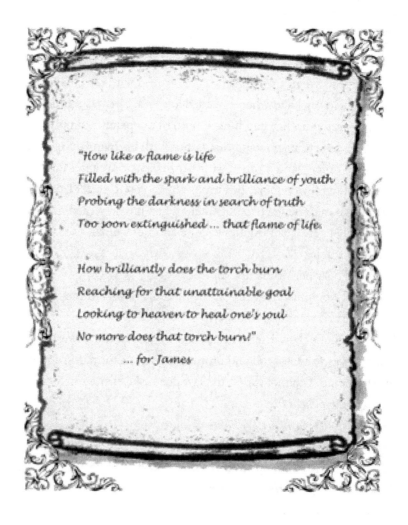

"How like a flame is life
Filled with the spark and brilliance of youth
Probing the darkness in search of truth
Too soon extinguished ... that flame of life.

How brilliantly does the torch burn
Reaching for that unattainable goal
Looking to heaven to heal one's soul
No more does that torch burn!"

                    ... for James

Her words betrayed a secret sorrow, so unlike her usual joy for life. Now her promise would never be fulfilled, her youth would never mature, and her laughter silenced forever. And the dedication: "for James", a mystery that I was not to solve until sometime later, when I searched for the truth of her death.

I loved my sister with all the passion of a young, adoring brother.

Watching the interment of my dear sister had the curious effect of stirring old memories from my early childhood. I was barely seven years old when I had been taken down to the east end of London, either by my father or my uncle, I can't remember just who it was.

We entered an antiquated curiosity shop, originally established many years ago, before that neighborhood had fallen into desperate times. The shop had deteriorated into an establishment of oddities and freaks of nature.

I entered the shop and immediately to my left was confronted by a glass cage containing a two-headed snake! The sign on the top of the cage read "Danger! Janus Viper" – a two-headed snake named after the two-headed god of ancient Rome, who could see the future and the past at the same time. Of the Janus Viper, one head was devoid of any venom, the other filled with a double dose of deadly poisonous venom, so concentrated that it was instantly lethal!

It seemed as if the lethal head had assumed the role of protector of the non-poisonous one, instinctively recognizing it was all part of one hideous creature pitted against the forces of nature; an example of an oddity of nature adapting to survive.

I felt it was a capricious jest of nature that one head was completely deprived of the life-protecting supply of venom, while the other seemed to have inherited a double dose, as if possessing what should have been equally distributed between the two of them. This inequity of inheritance rendered one side a harmless pet, while the other a doubly lethal threat to life. Had the vipers been formed in two complete halves, a new variety of snake may have been born.

While I looked with fascinated interest at the paradoxical viper in its glass case, a beautiful lady walked into the shop. I remember thinking how poised and proper she appeared.

Walking over to the owner of the shop, she handed him a pair of especially designed wedding rings saying: "How much can I get for these? I have no use for them any longer!"

The shop owner studied them for a moment and then gave her a price. All at once, the countenance of the lady changed. She screamed at him, "You miserable cheat! They are worth much more than that!" The argument built to a fever pitch. There were words being spoken that I didn't quite understand.

Then, the furious lady grabbed the rings and stormed out of the shop, slamming the door behind her. The violent transformation of so beautiful a lady into a vicious, menacing creature somehow became mixed with the vision of the two-headed snake; a picture of gentleness mixed with life-threatening ferociousness within the same body.

This experience of a seven-year-old boy became confused with an impression of the dual nature of women – at one time a fascinating, harmless creature and then, suddenly a threat of doom. Why this fixation remained in my memory I do not know. But as time passed and I grew toward manhood, the particulars of the experience faded into the deep recesses of memory, while the metaphor persisted on to affect my relationship or more precisely, my non-relationship with women.

I was pulled out of my thoughts by the doleful chiming of the chapel bells of St. Mary's of Lead Church. It was a small, simple building in Yorkshire County. I had been christened here and the Holmes family had attended Sunday services in the old chapel for a number of generations.

It was a stone structure with beamed ceiling overlooking two small rows of pews, separated by a narrow aisle. Dating back to the medieval times, the chapel was the last vintage of the great manor house of Lead Hall, a majestic estate which had fallen into disrepair when it became too expensive to maintain. Now, there was nothing left but the tiny chapel, standing alone, as if to defy the encroaching world outside. It was a timeless world within itself, for once the old timber doors were closed, I felt as if I were miles away from anywhere. Ghosts of the past came buzzing 'round my head, filling my mind with thoughts of long ago.

Reverend Josiah Pendleton broke the silence with his incantation.

"As one generation passeth away, another cometh to take its place. But when the younger generation proceeds, who shall follow? And yet, surely, the earth abideth forever!"

After the blessing, the congregation, no more than a small gathering of family members and friends, now moved outside to the chapel cemetery and gravesite. The procession followed behind the simple, unadorned casket.

The rain had not stopped and, indeed, nature seemed to be providing a fitting atmospheric chorus to underscore the mournful rituals of the day. As we stood around the casket, the raindrops blended with the bitter tears on my cheeks, falling to the ground in a pool of sorrow at my feet. I truly believe that the hardest thing in life is the loss of a loved one.

A canopy decorated with her favorite flowers had been erected to give some protection from the unkind weather. A random cluster of assorted umbrellas formed the irregular pattern of a second canopy, giving shelter to most of the crowd, which had assembled to mourn my sister's untimely death. The rain persisted.

Reverend Pendleton spoke at the ceremony.

"Dearly beloved, we are gathered here in sorrow and in hope to wish our lately departed sister of the church, Violet-Rose Holmes, a safe and swift journey to our heavenly father. Now all of life's vanities fall away. Ashes to ashes, dust to dust. May she rest in peace with the Lord above."

Now, the rain began to fall in torrents, forcing an abrupt and cruel end to the ceremonies. Nature had decreed that the ceremony for my sister would be carried out without any element of serenity, grace, or dignity. Fate would have its own way!

The guests made a mad dash for the cabs and carriages that had been provided for their journey to the reception that was planned at our country home. Some refreshments had been prepared for them.

I desperately searched for any empty cab, when one pulled up beside me.

"Come in out of the rain, brother," the voice of Mycroft, my older brother, called out.

I quickly climbed into the shelter of his two-seated Hansom Cab and signaled the coachman to drive off for home.

As we drove off, I took one last look back and saw the grave caretakers struggling to close the coffin lid and proceeding with the interment of my sister into the grave. It sickened my soul to think of her in the corrupting ground.

I tried to bury that memory by beginning a conversation with my brother.

But Mycroft began the conversation first!

"It's been quite a while since we've had a chance to talk," were his initial words.

"Yes," I replied. We embraced. "The family has been split apart for some time now," I replied. "We have plenty to discuss."

"You were always closer to Violet-Rose than I ever was!"

His remark stirred up a flood of early childhood memories.

"Yes, brother, but I remember those days when we all were close. You two used to read to me from the stories of Tennyson's tales of King Arthur. Each one of you took parts --- she the damsel in distress, and you the gallant knight who came to the rescue! I was but a little child then, and I loved you both."

Mycroft hesitated for a moment, and then spoke.

"Yes, but everything has changed. Life has gotten more complicated. The family has grown more distant from each other and, as we have grown, we each have taken separate paths, pulling away from our center. The simple, happy days are no more!" he sighed.

Then, with unaccustomed emotion, he blurted out a warning I never forgot.

"Lock up your heart, brother. Guard against sentimentality, Sherlock! It's the only way to survive life's capriciousness."

"Yes," I sighed. "The rhythm of the universe is inscrutable! And who could have known that our sister's downfall would come as a result of her appetite for sweet chocolates?"

"Chocolates?" questioned Mycroft.

"Yes, a corrupted molar tooth was the cause of it all!" I recalled.

"Quite so," said Mycroft. "I remember now that father insisted on taking her to that new dentist touring London … a certain Doctor Thomas Evans."

"He was an American, wasn't he?" I replied.

"Yes. He boasted a new painless method of tooth extraction introduced by Doctor Horus Wells, a few years earlier. You know how Violet-Rose feared pain! Father wanted nothing but the best for her," observed Mycroft.

"Well, the extraction went without problem," I remembered. "But the post-operative pain had to be treated."

"Yes," said Mycroft, "with Paracelsus Laudanum, a cocktail composed largely of opium and alcohol."

"And addiction to opium came quickly, I remember. She sought more of the drug from any source she could get."

"What happened after that?" asked Mycroft. "I was off to London on a mission for the service."

"Well, eventually she fell in with an unsavory group of scoundrels and, taking advantage of her dependency, they dragged her down into the gutter of depravity."

I stopped to wipe away a tear.

"My sister," I said, painfully. "She, who showed such brilliance and promise in her youth, changed and became distant, withdrawn and depressed."

Now, the rain came down even more fiercely than before. As the deluge beat down upon the roof of the cab, the noise made conversation impossible. So, we just sat there in silence as we rode to the Holmes country estate at Elmwood Hall.

It was at least an hour's ride to our home. By then the thunderous downpour had subsided. In its place came the warm sunshine and, to belie the maliciousness of the inconvenient cloud burst, there appeared a rainbow in the sky!

The place where we called home was a modest country house befitting our father's status as a country squire. The estate sat at the end of a long elm and chestnut tree-lined drive. In addition to wooded areas, ponds and gardens, there were areas left untamed to encourage the wildlife, which included an abundance of deer, foxes, rabbits, and badgers; a veritable playground for me in my childhood.

However, now the long pathway that led up to the hall betrayed a dangerous condition of neglect. As we approached the house, broken pieces of the flagstone pathway crumbled beneath our feet. The building itself was in an embarrassing state of disrepair. The workmen had been dismissed some time ago, as the cost of improvements could not be afforded in these recent times.

Mycroft, having been away from the homestead, remarked, "What a shameful condition our family home has sunken into, Sherlock!"

"Yes, father's income is not what it used to be since he was dismissed from government service," I replied, somewhat embarrassed. "Many things are not as they should be since mother is gone!"

We entered through the large oak doors and came upon a spacious sitting room. The ceiling was wood-beam and plaster. The large fireplace gave warmth to the occasion that was greatly appreciated. The sitting room accommodated not only the immediate family who had come together, but also a few guests.

A large painting depicting a hunting scene hung over the fireplace and on either side were mounted the stately heads of two large stags. They were said to have been shot by previous members of the Holmes family. A large area rug covered the slate floor, giving some protection from the uncomfortable dampness that was an inevitable consequence of the weather.

A shield with the Holmes coat of arms hung on the wall. On it were a lion rampant crest, three bugle horns on the shield proper, and the motto beneath: "Just and firm of purpose."

Engraved under the Holmes coat of arms was the saying: "Give alms from thy goodness and turn not thy face from any poor man and the face of the Lord shall not be turned from thee!"

Father stood by the fireplace and addressed the assemblage. "It appears that the fortunes of the Holmes family are at low ebb. But for the achievements of our son, Mycroft, the family finds itself in sad decline. With the death of Violet-Rose, the family has suffered a great tragedy."

He continued on. "And another misfortune has arisen to plague us. Our ancestral home, Elmwood Hall, will be sold within the month. The crushing taxes, brought about by the current agricultural depression in England, have all but bankrupted us."

A gasp came from the crowd.

Father continued. "We will drink a last toast to the family Holmes. Are all the glasses charged?"

Mycroft stood up and brought father a glass of port wine.

"Here, father, take this and lead our toast!"

All of a sudden, *Bang!* A loud shot rang out in the house. The bullet whistled past Mycroft's ear and lodged squarely in father's forehead, killing him instantly. A woman screamed and all the guests dived to the floor for cover.

"What is happening?" I thought.

Then I saw someone running toward the large oak doors. He struggled to push them open.

"There's the assassin!" I cried and bolted after him. He scampered quickly down the flagstone path with me in pursuit.

"I'm coming," yelled Mycroft, just behind me.

The assassin was quick-footed and would probably have escaped had it not been for a bit of luck. The man caught his foot on some of the crumbled flagstone and fell to the ground. He yelled in pain, having twisted his ankle. The rifle he carried flew out of his grasp and landed some distance away. I caught up with him and pinned him to the ground.

"I've got you, you villain!"

Mycroft was at my heels.

"Hold him, Sherlock, while I summon the constable."

Among the guests at the church was Inspector Lestrade, a friend of Mycroft. The constable came running, and quickly snapped a pair of handcuffs on our murderer, who was writhing in pain, his ankle having swollen up to twice its size.

Lestrade proceeded to interrogate him. "I know you, Vincent Moran, of the notorious Moran brothers. You work for a mysterious, unknown criminal. Hired assassins! Ruthless killers! You are the terror of all London!"

The man was in such pain that I almost felt sorry for him! But he had murdered father and would pay for his horrible deed.

Mycroft added to the story. "I've been investigating his scurvy gang on drug smuggling charges!"

"Drug smuggling?" I asked, astonished.

"Yes, there has been an increase in the illegal importing of drugs into England. We have known about it for some time, but never have we been able to get enough evidence on the culprits to arrest them. Now we have one of the brothers on a murder charge and soon we will have them all."

The miserable man spoke up. "You'll never catch my brother, Sebastian, nor our leader, James ..."

The man stopped short of naming the mysterious criminal mastermind.

Lestrade looked at Mycroft.

"I'm afraid he's right. I don't see how we can implicate those two master criminals in the drug-dealing activity."

The man spoke up again, directing his threat to Mycroft.
"I missed you today, but there will be other days and other men.
You are a marked man!"

So, father had died needlessly as a result of the criminal's poor aim!

Mycroft shrugged off the threat, but I saw the danger to my brother
and felt some intervention must be made on his behalf.

"We're dealing with a criminal mastermind. He has been behind
a large part of the criminal activity around London for some time!"
said Mycroft. "We've tried to apprehend the villain, but he always slips
through our fingers."

The wretched prisoner spoke up from his place on the ground. "You'll
never catch him. We've all pledged our lives to protect him!"

"Quiet, you villain," shouted Lestrade. "There won't be anyone to protect you!"

Arrangements were made for father's funeral and burial next to Violet-Rose.

The Reverend Pendleton spoke the words.

"Father in heaven, what has this family done to merit such tragedy?
Will this misfortune, which has afflicted the Holmes family, now lead to
their ultimate demise?"

The words fell hard on my ears, but what could be done?

I cried out. "Have we not endured enough?"

My feelings turned from sorrow to anger, and that anger gave me
purpose. It was up to me then, Sherlock Holmes, to take up the gauntlet
and accept the challenge of solving the double mystery of my father's and
sister's murders. Because of the dedication "… for James" at the end of
her last poem, I had deduced that, at one of those drug frolics, my sister
had been there seeking to satisfy her drug craving brought on by the laudanum she had taken. There was no doubt that this "James" had sought to
make her one of his "opium slaves" obedient to his every whim. She had
been caught in the web of destruction that this insane monster had spun
in his quest for world power.

The next step was to determine where and when the upcoming "Drug Party" was to be held. After inflicting some painful persuasion on our prisoner, we convinced him to tell us the particulars about the next drug party. I volunteered to go in disguise as a young, wayward tramp to infiltrate the debauchery, over Mycroft's protests.

"This is no picnic, Sherlock. You could be killed!"

But I reminded him of his advice to me.

"Lock up your heart, brother. Guard against sentimentality. It's the only way to survive life's capriciousness!"

Mycroft did not take my chiding well.

"Heart be damned! This is an occasion for the head. And my head tells me that you will suffer greatly for this reckless escapade!" was his stinging reply.

Despite his misgivings the plan was to be carried out. Two weeks later, I was in disguise and wandered into the "frolic." Men and women were getting a high from the nitrous oxide provided for the entertainment. I pretended to inhale some of the gas and acted my part. When the guests were wildly intoxicated, the gang began to inject the victims with morphine and cocaine doses to begin their addiction.

As the party grew wilder, I looked for their mysterious leader, but he had kept to the shadows, watching with malevolent enthusiasm.

The plan was that I should send a signal out to Lestrade and his men. But when I thought the proper time had arrived, I tried to whistle loudly to give the signal. However, some of the nitrous oxide had gotten to me and dulled my wits. I just could not whistle! Suddenly, a villainous man stepped into the open and motioned to two very strong ruffians.

"Grab him!" he ordered.

I was in their grasp and could not escape!

"Sherlock Holmes the meddler, Sherlock Holmes the amateur, Sherlock Holmes the bungler," came his taunting words. "You are caught in the spider's web. We missed your brother, but his time will come when he least expects it. Now, you will feel the spider's sting ... the venom of cocaine." He laughed an evil laugh and beckoned to a third gang member, who forcibly injected into my arm the carefully prepared dose of seven percent solution of cocaine. I tried to remember his face, but everything was a blur.

My mind exploded with an intensity that was overpowering. I was experiencing the first taste of drug intoxication … the spider's sting! It was a condition that would be with me for the rest of my life. I would go on battling cocaine dependence despite all my efforts to control it. My bouts with addiction would forever haunt me.

Fortunately, Inspector Lestrade had decided to crash the party without waiting for my signal. There was a lot of yelling and pushing. Finally, the police had all the suspects in handcuffs … all, that is, except for their venomous leader, the black spider, who had remained nameless. He and Moran had carefully planned their escape in the event that they were raided.

"Gone again!" yelled Mycroft, in disappointment. Then he came to me.

"Brother, are you alright?" he asked, worriedly.

But I was not all right! My head buzzed like a swarm of bees. My lips were too thick to respond to his question.

"I was afraid of this!" shouted Mycroft, both furious and helpless. "All because of your recklessness! Will you ever learn?"

As I lay in a drug-induced stupor, Mycroft tended me night and day. Finally, my brain began to clear. It took a number of days for me to regain some sense of normalcy.

"How long have I been here, brother?" I asked.

Mycroft breathed a sigh of relief.

"Three days, Sherlock. Three days of hideous nightmares!"

"What happened after the party?" I asked.

"Well, every one of the gang was caught, and the local drug gang was smashed. But its mysterious leader was nowhere to be found."

"Probably off scheming to commit some other heinous crime against an unsuspecting public," I interrupted.

"Relax, brother, he will have his turn," said Mycroft. "Oh, by the way, he left a note for you."

"A note!" I said, not knowing what to expect.

"Here, read it!"

I took the note into my shaky hands.

Dear Sherlock,

Greetings to   my foolish Sleuth

Who prowls the Night in Search of truth.

Intently does he   Hunt his prey,

While the Man of Mystery steels away!

To understand   The Evil Mind

Is very Difficult You'll find

For when you think you've Solved the crime

He'll just outwit you   Every time

You've come against the King of crime

You'll find you cannot Win this Time.

I leave you to   Your Sweet cocaine

I hope it drives   You quite Insane!

Yours truly, ...James

The taunting letter fired my spirit.

"Why that ..."

"Calm down, Sherlock, you need your rest now. There will be another time for vengeance," counseled Mycroft.

As I got over the stinging sarcasm of the rhyme, I decided to determine a profile of the man who wrote it. I could not remember much of the details of the party and so could not identify my antagonist. His face was a blur, but I could remember his evil laugh.

In my earlier days I had become interested in the organization of my observational talents under two disciplines: induction and deduction.

I used them together to solve a problem. The discipline of induction moved from specific observations to broad generalizations, a bottom-up approach. This helped to deal with everyday problems that depend on partial information to solve them. Whereas, deduction, a top-down approach, led from general premises to specific conclusions. By using a combination of both induction to form a general theory, and then deductive thinking to test the theory with observations of the facts, I had become very successful in my early attempts at problem solving.

I had gotten interested in studying the analysis of handwriting. By induction, I had formulated a theory that certain details of the formulation of the individual calligraphic characteristics of the letters and word grouping betrayed definite personality inclinations. Therefore, the smallest details of a sample of handwriting would serve as an open window to a person's mind.

The openness of the letters, the angularity of the strokes, and even the peculiar way that the pen was held cradled in the hand, along with the dexterity of the fingers, all surrendered their own clues to the author's personality, attitudes, and life style.

Having arrived at this premise early on, I studied the letters that were hastily written on the note and used deductive reasoning to test the premise.

"And what do you propose to do with that piece of nonsense?" inquired Mycroft, in half jest and half curiosity.

"I shall discover the character of our criminal mastermind, my dear brother," I responded.

"How on earth do you propose to do that Sherlock? Do you think the paper will speak to you of its owner?"

"It will speak!" I answered, determined to let the words talk to me in their own special way.

My brother, Mycroft, was possessed of a brilliant mind, more brilliant than mine, I suspect. But his brilliance had sometimes blinded him to certain circumstances of everyday life. Living in his rarefied world he often displayed an insufferable arrogance.

I have often recalled that my early study of handwriting had come over the objections of others who thought it a foolish waste of time. But I have long since shielded myself against the foolish detractions of their petty minds!

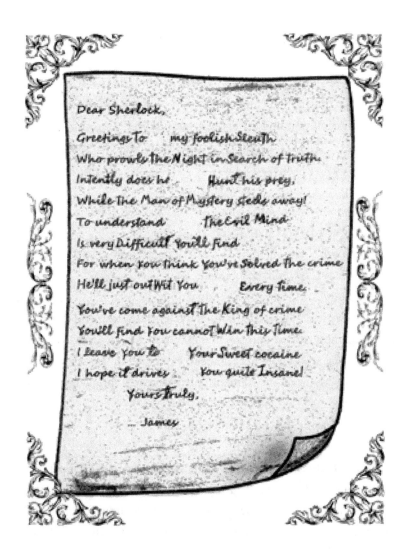

And now the letter …

Although the initial cursory scanning of the letter had revealed a biting indictment of my poor detection skills, which I have endeavored to correct over time, a rereading with a more detached and critical observation of the technical details of the individual written letters revealed an enlightening characterization of the author's personality – a very definite criminal profile.

"Let me see … the letters tend to disconnect and are not slanted but point straight up. That, of course, identifies him as an abstract thinker --- the indication that he is a very self-confident mastermind. Now the long-stemmed "Y" with a sharply upturned tail belies his deeply aggressive nature. And of course, the looped "T" indicates his suspicious nature."

"What are you talking about?" snapped Mycroft.

"It has been used since the time of Aristotle!" I replied.

"What has?" Mycroft snapped.

"Graphology!" I answered.

"What-ology?" Mycroft responded.

"Graphology … the study of handwriting," I explained. "Every individual's handwriting has a style and character of its own and this is due to the uniqueness of that person's mental characteristics. Handwriting is the pattern of our psychological makeup expressed in the symbols on the page, and these symbols are quite unique and readily predictable," I said in frustration.

"Really?" responded Mycroft.

"Well," I said, trying to remain calm, "graphology not only reveals a person's personality, but also his psychological problems, even conditions under which an individual has grown up. Characteristics of strength and anger eventually determine the physicality of his handwriting. The age, gender, and dominant hand of a writer can also be determined, if studied carefully. Now let me finish my analysis!"

I went back to the piece of paper.

"Where was I? Oh yes! The large size letters indicate a need to be noticed and a lust for power. The looped "T" signifies that he takes criticism harshly. And the boldness of the letters confirms this. Then, the wide loop of the "L" indicates big dreams and goals --- to the extremes of megalomania. Finally, the unnecessary use of capitals and uneven spacing of the letters is the sign of a sociopath … definite criminal insanity!"

"You got all that from looking at the character of the letters?" said Mycroft, in amazement.

"Elementary, Mycroft, simply elementary, my dear brother!" I said with satisfaction.

By the end of the month, the family estate was sold for taxes, and I was looking for lodgings. London seemed to be the best place to locate, since I could be close to Mycroft and could continue my search for the unknown mastermind criminal who had disrupted my once orderly life.

Of course, I had to discontinue my studies at the university, so I decided to inform my chemistry professor of my intentions. Professor Joseph Belmont was like a great uncle to me. Many hours were spent after class discussing exotic drugs and poisons that had come to hold a fascination for me.

"I feel I must put my studies behind me," I told him with emphatic candor.

He tried to dissuade me. "You were always so interested in the chemical sciences," he insisted. "I thought you would never give them up."

"Not give them up," I corrected, "for I mean to put them to practical use now!"

"Use, how?" he questioned.

"Yes, professor. I shall use my knowledge to seek out the truth concerning my father's and sister's deaths. Their lives were snuffed out so viciously by some unscrupulous devils. I mean to find them out and end their treacherous ways!"

"But you would sacrifice a budding career for vengeance … the act of a fool, my boy!"

I replied in anger. "No, not a boy, but the act of a loving brother and son, to salvage their honor from the condemnation of a world's corruptness. A true gentleman always protects his family's honor!"

"So, you would take up the challenge at all costs," he said, amazed by my tenacity.

"Yes," I replied emphatically, "and justice will be done! I have decided to devote my life and my abilities to the task of solving crime!"

"I admire your dedication, Sherlock. Then use it for searching out the clues."

He put his hand on my shoulder. "Go then, and God be with you!"

I left my old professor, not knowing if I would ever hear his encouraging voice again.

I had struck out on my own in search of an enigma … Who was this mysterious criminal mastermind who had caused so much pain and bitterness in my life?

But first things first! I found employment at St. Bartholomew's Hospital working in the chemistry lab. Then, I rented a room at a private hotel. But my finances soon dictated that I leave there and find a less expensive place to live. I determined that I might inquire about lodgings elsewhere by frequenting the Criterion Bar and Restaurant. I had been told that it was a gathering place for persons of rather good reputation. If I could meet someone and start up a conversation about available places at a reasonable price, then my immediate troubles would be over.

Sure enough, I soon met an amiable fellow, named Stamford, who, in the course of conversation let me know of a certain Dr. John Watson, who wished to share the cost of lodgings with a congenial flat mate.

The doctor and I met, and, after establishing some particulars of compatibility, decided to get together the next day at No. 221B Baker Street to finalize our agreement. The landlady, Mrs. Hudson, was satisfied with our arrangement of each paying half the rent and sharing the apartment space.

As the weeks went by, we settled into a life of bachelorhood, learning each other's habits and necessities. Watson was a prince of a man … considerate, free of guile, and professed to enjoying my violin playing (although that may have been a concession for the sake of compatibility), and he suffered my bouts with cocaine in tasteful silence.

One evening, as we sat by the fireplace, Dr. Watson brought up the subject of my plans for the future. I told him of the murders of my father and sister. He was stunned.

"What vicious crimes, Holmes!"

"Yes," I replied. "I have devoted my life to the search for the mysterious criminal who perpetrated the evil deeds. In my heart I have a premonition that someday we will meet face to face for a final reckoning, and justice will at last be done!"

There was an immediate comfort to our relationship ... almost like the feel of an old pair of shoes, or the last piece of a puzzle, which, when put in place, formed a perfect fit to complete the picture of a long and lasting friendship. I began to feel as if I had found a new brother --- Dr. John Watson and I, Sherlock Holmes.

ADVENTURE NO. 2
The Severed Hand
FROM A SECRET CASE FILE OF SHERLOCK HOLMES

The Severed Hand
From a Secret Case File of Sherlock Holmes

I
t was a colder winter than I had known for at least a decade. The warmth of the fire gave a glow appropriate to the season. I had invited a guest for Christmas dinner, for, in truth, I needed the company to raise my spirits. I had lost a friend, my illustrious acquaintance, that irritating practitioner of logic, that genius of detection; in a word, Sherlock Holmes.

In the time since his death at the hands of his mortal enemy, Professor Moriarty, life had changed. Since that incident at Reichenbach Falls, there was an emptiness that seemed impossible to fill, a finality that was impossible to accept, a loneliness that was too heavy to bear.

Staring into the crackling fireplace, the sparks burst into the air and flickered in a moment of brilliance. But just as quickly, they receded into the dark recesses of the hearth. How like old memories that burst into the forefront of our thoughts and for a brief moment seem more real than the present. An old letter had stirred the embers of events long ago and I was lost in thought. My memories soon faded into the dimness of the past and I was called back by a knock on the door. I hastily stuffed the letter back into my pocket.

"It is I, Doctor Watson," came the familiar friendly voice.

I got up from my chair and moved as quickly as my old bones would allow. "Coming, Doctor Watson." Opening the door, I perceived the good-natured smile of a man who was determined to bring a cheerful countenance to our meeting. "Happy Christmas, Doctor. Come in and warm yourself before dinner."

"Happy Christmas, Mrs. Hudson. It was so nice of you to invite me to Christmas dinner; just the occasion for old friends to exchange pleasantries. I've brought you a gift to warm your heart ... a bottle of fine sherry."

"Thank you, how good of you." He brushed off a bit of snow remaining on his collar. As it fell to the floor, he looked apologetically at me. "I'm sorry, Mrs. Hudson, I didn't mean to soil the carpet."

I smiled. "That's all right. I don't worry as much about those things now. I guess it's a legacy from Mr. Holmes."

He suddenly turned pensive and melancholy. "Yes, we all have our legacies to live with." Then he pulled out his pocket watch. "I trust I am on time. Don't want to spoil the dinner, you know."

"We have plenty of time … all evening in fact. So don't worry about a thing." I opened the bottle and poured him some of the Christmas sherry, he had so thoughtfully brought. Then I noticed that he stood staring at his pocket watch for a moment. I recognized the likeness of his dear departed wife within the cover. "She was a beautiful person, Doctor."

"Yes, like a delicate flower tossed in the wind." He fought to control the tears welling up in his eyes. "The flu epidemic swept through London and took her from me, you know. She was always visiting the hospitals doing charitable works for the old and sick. She said it was her joy to help those less fortunate in life."

"There, there, now Doctor, you must keep the good memories. They're the things that sustain us in times of sorrow." I hoped my words were of some comfort to him. The poor man had just recently lost his friend and companion, Mr. Holmes, and his dear wife, Mary. He was doubly alone. The bonds of love and friendship were severed forever.

"You're right, of course. I mustn't dwell on the past." He put his watch back in his pocket.

His words sent a flood of memories through my mind. "Sometimes I think back to the days when my dear husband, Edward, was still with me. He was a soldier, you know; decorated for gallant action during the foreign campaigns."

The doctor's expression changed from melancholy to surprise. "I didn't know. You never mention him."

"Oh yes, he was awarded the *British Waterloo Medal* and later the *Victoria Cross*."

I struggled to gain my composure. "Yes, but he is always with me … as Mary will be with you, Doctor."

"Your husband's name was Edward?"

"Yes, Edward Matthew Hudson."

"Tell me, Mrs. Hudson what is your Christian name? You have never spoken it in all our time together."

"Martha Marie."

"Martha Marie Hudson?"

"Yes, but I never use it now. It reminds me too much of the old days. I prefer just Mrs. Hudson."

"Well, Mrs. Hudson, to what shall we drink our first Christmas toast?"

"Since we are met here in his very room, it seems appropriate to raise our glasses to Sherlock Holmes."

We raised our glasses. "To the incomparable and enigmatic Mr. Holmes." The sherry brought a warmth to our spirits and conversation came easier. "I still can't believe he is really gone. I still visit his room every day, although it is no longer in the hopelessly disheveled state that he was pleased to leave it in."

Watson laughed out loud. "He certainly set a task for you, didn't he? You were a saint! I confess that sometimes even I approached the limits of my patience with him."

I remembered Mr. Holmes' disdain for neatness. "So, like the son that Edward and I never had. I really didn't mind picking up after him … that is, when he allowed me to do so. But I realized that his great mind was wrestling with so many complex problems that he simply could not attend to the ordinary … that everyday boredom of living. It was no great trouble to help out, especially when we first met."

The doctor's eyebrows lifted with curiosity. "You knew Holmes before I met him?"

"Oh yes. He was deeply troubled about conditions in the London community and was always seeking to 'weed out the garden,' as he put it, of the criminal element. In fact, Mr. Holmes solved his first important case as a result of his seeking lodging here."

"You never told me that!" Doctor Watson's eyes flashed with excitement. "Please in heaven's name, do tell me the details."

We settled back in our comfortable chairs and continued with
the story.

"Yes, what a curious first meeting. It's an event I'm not likely to forget.
I remember I was doing some last-minute cleaning before the arrival of a
potential lodger for this room. His credentials were impeccable and I had
all but decided that he was the right choice.

"Then came a knock at the door. I remember it was a rather substan-
tial, yet impatient knock, not what I had expected from the lodger who
had applied for the room. There was a second knock and I hurried to
the door. I could hardly have known that once I opened the door my life
would be forever changed.

"'Yes, yes, I'm coming'. I opened the door and before me stood a tall
man, well over six feet, a rather thin figure of a man, carelessly attired in
a well-worn suit of clothes. His eyes were piercing and alert, nose rather
hawk-like. His square chin gave him a very determined look. He appeared to be in his late 20's or early 30's."

"Mrs. Hudson?" His sharp eyes took in every detail of my appearance
at once. "I see that you have been cleaning in preparation for a new lodger,
as evidenced by the feather duster still on the mantle and the absolutely
perfect arrangement of the knickknacks on the end tables."

"What a remarkable statement!" Then he continued with an explanation, as if to settle my apprehension.

"You see, it is really quite a simple task to connect one set of inferences
to another and so to construct a chain of deduction that must lead from
the first observation to the final conclusion. If one then eliminates the
intervening links of the chain and presents only the first juxtaposed with
the last, we create the appearance of an astonishing feat of intellectual
prowess, which is, in fact, merely a simple step-by-step journey that much
resembles the mundane task of climbing up a flight of stairs."

I was not sure how to answer him.

"My name is Sherlock Holmes. You have been recommended to me by a friend, Stamford, as a woman in need of a lodger and, since I am a lodger in need of a room, I have decided to make myself available to your establishment."

I hesitated at the boldness of his presentment. "Oh, but I have already considered another lodger."

"You mean the rather dull chap waiting at the doorway downstairs? I told him that the room was already taken. You wouldn't have approved of him, anyway, rather pompous and fastidious."

So intense was his attitude and yet so genuinely forthright and impressive, that I felt strangely comfortable with Mr. Holmes. "My dear lady, I merely wish to rent your room. It is important that I do so for private reasons. I assure you my needs are few and I shall endeavor to keep to myself as much as possible Unfortunately, my funds are limited, but I could share the expenses with a certain Dr. Watson, whom I have just met. He will be here tomorrow to close our arrangement."

I regained my composure and gestured courteously but cautiously. "Come in Mr. Holmes. You look like a fine young gentleman, but you know a woman must be careful, nowadays, with ruffians and unsavory types frequenting the streets."

"Oh yes, I am well aware of the shroud of evil that hangs over our poor city like a malevolent mist."

"Well, I dare say it's not that bad, Mr. Holmes, but one must be on guard, of course." I didn't wish to seem too alarmist to the young man.

"Oh, but you are right my good woman. The depths of evil cannot really be appreciated until one has lifted the veil of respectability and peeked beneath the surface of our fine British façade."

"Whatever do you mean, Mr. Holmes?"

"Forgive me, Mrs. Hudson. I should warn you that I am intimately associated with crimes … solving them, not committing them!"

I wondered if I had made a mistake by giving this young man so generous a welcome. "Indeed, Mr. Holmes, I hope that you will not endanger my establishment. I have been a widow for some years now and I have managed to keep my reputation and the reputation of my house free of any scandal or impropriety."

But before I could consider the matter any further, our discussion was interrupted by the hysterical entrance of my friend, Mrs. Warren, who ran the boarding house just down the street.

"Oh, Mrs. Hudson. Whatever shall I do? I think they're killing him!"

Mr. Holmes spoke up with such authority that we both stood in silence. "Dear lady, calm yourself and tell me just the pertinent facts … and for heaven's sake be quick about it."

I sensed that he had experienced this kind of emergency before and was comfortable, and, in truth, quite excited by the prospect of becoming involved in such a potentially dangerous affair.

Mrs. Warren quickly told us of the gruesome events which were, at that very moment, occurring at her boarding house. One of her tenants, a bizarre man named Trayer was in the habit of keeping some very strange pets in his room. These "little pets", as he called them, were deadly piranha fish that he had brought up from the jungles of South America. He said he kept them there in a large tank because they made him feel safe. "Sentinels at the gate" is what he called them. It made no sense to anyone! "Sentinels at the gate"?

Then Mrs. Warren quickly continued her story as coherently as she could. "But just a few minutes ago, three men came up to his room and then began shouting and yelling, the likes of which I have never heard. Mr. Trayer was screaming something about his fish, when one of those horrible men began laughing with so vicious and evil a tone that I just ran out of the house and came right here."

Mr. Holmes shot into action. "There is no time to lose. A great evil is being done."

Mrs. Warren pointed out the location of her boarding house and he ran out straight for it.

Doctor Watson could contain himself no longer. "Holmes was always charging headlong into danger without a care for his own safety."

"Yes, Doctor Watson, that was Mr. Holmes' way," I agreed.

The dear doctor was impatient for an answer that I was not able to give. "What happened next? Did Holmes get there in time?"

"Good heavens, Mrs. Hudson, I must know the truth of it!"

As if in answer to his entreaty, there was a knock at the door. "Now, who can that be, Doctor? I'm not expecting any other guests tonight!" I opened the door and there stood …

"Happy Christmas, Mrs. Hudson."

"Mr. Mycroft Holmes! My word!" I overcame my surprise and remembering my duties as hostess invited him in. "You know Dr. Watson?"

"Of course. Happy Christmas, Doctor."

"Happy Christmas. What an honor to meet you here."

"Well, I just came around to see that Sherlock's things are still in order and to offer Mrs. Hudson a little sum to cover the expenses."

It was the first time that Mycroft had come down to see his younger brother's apartment. I usually received his recompense by postal delivery. I sensed a special reason for his visit. "It really is so wonderful of you to cover the costs of keeping Mr. Holmes' apartment as a memorial."

"I prefer to think of it as a living memory."

I had never thought of Mycroft as an emotional person, but he seemed uneasy at his pronouncement. It was as if he wanted to say more, but felt it was better left unsaid.

Then he changed the subject. "By the way Doctor Watson, I have never fully expressed my admiration for the gift that you and your wife, Mary, bequeathed to the London hospitals for the poor."

Doctor Watson beamed proudly. "It was entirely her decision, you know."

"Yes, it was quite remarkable how she unselfishly gave away her small fortune to help the hospitals of London."

I turned to the doctor in surprise. "Why Doctor, I had not heard about Mary's gift. You have been keeping your own secret story from me."

Doctor Watson laughed, somewhat embarrassed. "Well, do you remember that Mary had received six beautiful pearls from that Sholto brother, Thaddeus? You know in that adventure that I called the *Sign of Four?*"

I knew that part of the story. "I do remember it well. But I always wondered what happened to those beautiful pearls. It seemed that you didn't benefit from them at all."

"Oh, on the contrary, Mrs. Hudson, they were the cause of our reunion after that first encounter. Mary never felt right about the pearls. She said they were nothing but a curse to everyone who owned them. Then one day she asked for my help. (As if I could ever refuse her anything.) She decided to give the pearls away, one to each of six London hospitals that treated the poor and helpless.

"Well, I was attracted to Mary from the first moment I saw her. But Holmes warned me not to let my good judgment be biased by personal qualities. How like him. Holmes the automaton! Holmes the calculating machine! Holmes the cool non-romantic! And yet, I think he finally recognized that Mary was the exception. She was my very life. So, we searched out the most deserving hospitals and settled the fortune accordingly."

Mycroft interrupted. "It was a beautiful gallant gesture ... *a beau geste,* as it were."

Doctor Watson smiled. "Yes, and from that moment on I knew I could never leave her. And so, we were married."

Then he added sadly. "She was struck down with the flu while visiting the sick in those very hospitals ... one of life's sad ironies."

I felt I must lighten the mood. "Well, you are just in time to join Dr. Watson and I in a glass of Christmas cheer. What is your pleasure?"

Mycroft hesitated. "Would it be presumptuous of me, that is, would it be impolite to ask for a glass of Napoleon brandy?"

I laughed. "Not at all. Mr. Holmes had me keep a supply in the off chance that you might visit him. He knew your habits."

Mycroft took the glass. "Yes, I regret that I never gave my younger brother the opportunity to offer me a glass himself. Perhaps I should have seen him more often, but the best of intentions … you know?"

Then Doctor Watson seized the opportunity to return to the story of Mr. Holmes' first important case.

"Mycroft, before you arrived, Mrs. Hudson and I were just discussing your brother's first important case. We were puzzled about some of the details. What happened when your brother arrived at Mrs. Warren's boarding house?"

"Well, Doctor, I'm just the person to fill you in, although it must be in strictest confidence." Mycroft took a long, slow sip of brandy and began his account of the adventure.

"My brother had arrived on the scene just before Inspector Smithson and I got there. Evidently, there were three men who had come up to extract information from Trayer. The police had been tipped off about those unsavory scoundrels, and they had asked my help because there was some question about a mysterious secret treasure and its financial implications to the British government."

Doctor Watson shook his head. "This gets more baffling all the time."

"Yes, Doctor, and it nearly ended Sherlock's career before it started. When we arrived, he was in the death grip of a large brute of a man, named Bruno. He had almost squeezed the life out of him. Inspector Smithson shot three rounds into the man before he let go. Another man, Slythe, was making his getaway through a window of Trayer's second floor apartment. Unfortunately, in his haste he lost his balance and plunged to his death below."

Doctor Watson interrupted. "But what about Holmes?"

"He lay there for a few minutes trying to catch his breath. It seems that the two thugs were acting under the orders of a third man, a mysterious shadowy figure who slipped away. The police were never able to get their hands on him.

"As Sherlock regained his composure, he told me of the events that had just transpired. We surmised that the four men were confederates in an attempt to conceal an illegal financial venture … perhaps a treasure of some sort. However, Trayer had decided to double cross the others and take it for himself.

"Trayer, on the run from the other three, took lodging at Mrs. Warren's boarding house. But it was the fellow's bad luck that he was found out by his confederates. When all efforts to make him divulge the treasure's secret hiding place had failed, they turned to threats of death. We surmised that Bruno, the misshapen giant of a man, with a jagged scar on his face, had lifted Trayer off the ground and carried him over to the tank containing the deadly piranhas. At first, when only his fingers had touched the water, the hungry creatures must have leaped up and began stripping the flesh off leaving only a skeleton. The victim's agonizing screams sent Mrs. Warren running off for help."

Caught up in Mycroft's story, I interrupted with my part of the story. "Yes, and that was just when I was interviewing Mr. Holmes for this room. He dashed out to try to prevent the crime."

Mycroft looked at me coolly for interrupting his telling of the adventure. Then he patiently resumed his story.

"When Sherlock got there Trayer's entire hand had been stripped to the bone still bathed in a swirling cloud of blood, and the piranhas continued their savage feeding frenzy. The other two men had decided to escape before Trayer's screams brought the police, or we would have had a more difficult time subduing them as well. Sherlock attacked Bruno, and with a desperate blow to the bridge of the giant man's nose, forced him to drop Trayer to the floor. But by now the entire hand had been severed through the bone and its skeleton lay at the bottom of the tank."

Mycroft noticed that I was turning uncomfortably in my chair. "I'm sorry if this story is too offensive Mrs. Hudson."

"Not at all, Mycroft," I replied not able to tear myself from this description of horror.

Mycroft continued. "Trayer was bleeding profusely and screaming. 'The sentinels! The sentinels at the gate!' It sounded like the mad ravings of a nearly dead man.

"Then Bruno grabbed Sherlock by the neck. He struggled to get free. But like some hideous boa constrictor Bruno tightened his grip until my poor brother nearly lost consciousness. That was the moment Inspector Smithson and I arrived on the scene. Smithson barely saved Sherlock's life by firing the three rounds. The last one went right through the skull.

"The first words of my brother after he had recovered his faculties were typically Sherlock. 'And to what happy coincidence do I owe this rare meeting, Mycroft?'

"I held back a smile and answered dryly. 'Well, Sherlock, I happened to be in the neighborhood, and hearing the commotion, I reasoned who else could it be but my over-energetic brother getting himself into trouble again!'

"Trouble, indeed! The trouble of trying to prevent that savage deed. But I fear I was too late!"

"In truth, my brother was right. The wretched man was near death, having lay bleeding all this while. We managed to get a brief statement from him about some of the particulars of the crime and then he died. Three other policemen arrived on the scene, having heard the screams of Trayer. Together with Inspector Smithson they saw to it that the bodies of the thugs were taken to Scotland Yard morgue."

Interrupting his story, Mycroft turned to Doctor Watson. "We could have used your skills that day, my good Doctor."

But the Doctor bade Mycroft to continue. "Yes, yes, pray go on."

Mycroft was now content to divulge the secret of the great treasure of Napoleon. He eyed us both, and then, satisfied that he had our complete attention, plunged into his story.

"Well, as near as we could piece together from Trayer's dying statement and what we knew from the police and diplomatic files, the whole affair began in the last days of that dreaded despot, Napoleon Bonaparte. That over-confident, pint-sized piece of French pastry was actually convinced that he was the man of destiny chosen to be the next Alexander, Caesar and Charlemagne all rolled into one! He had once boasted, 'In five years, I shall be master of the world.' I tell you that villain had no honor. Twice, at the battles of the Nile and Trafalgar he deserted his men and fled back to France, without a thought of regret for the thousands of corpses he left behind. His only comment when he reached Paris was 'The emperor has never felt healthier!'"

Doctor Watson could not resist a display of British patriotism. "But we showed him, with the likes of Nelson and Wellington; good British stock, those men. They gave him a taste of British steel."

"Yes, Doctor, and finally, the island of Elba became his little kingdom in exile."

Mycroft hesitated for a moment, as if deciding whether to continue his story.

"At the risk of divulging more than I should," he said, "let us continue in strictest confidence, my friends."

"Of course," we replied.

"Well, you know, of course, about his first abdication and his sentencing, to rule on the island of Elba," continued Mycroft.

Dr. Watson replied, "I know what was written about it in the papers."

I responded, "My knowledge of it is rather meager, I'm afraid. Such distant matters are not my usual cup of tea!"

Mycroft continued.

"We treated him too kindly ... much too kindly."

"How so?" I asked, innocently.

"We set him up as a ruler of Elba! Imagine that, a king in his little kingdom," complained Mycroft. "We set the fox up in the henhouse! You see, there was no mechanism to bring a ruler of a country to trial! He was an emperor of France and had been commander of a powerful army!"

Mycroft grew more angry as he continued.

"Even when he went into exile on Elba, he was allowed to bring an administrative staff and a guard of 400 loyal men who followed him into exile. He even had the audacity to choose the island nation of Elba where he was to reign! Elba was only 40 miles from his native Corsica and 150 miles from France.

"He was also allowed to keep his title as Emperor! The victorious nations wanted to restrain him, not crush him. What a mistake! Although Napoleon submitted to their authority, he was planning to escape. And it was one of history's greatest prison breaks.

"This happened because Napoleon chose the island of Elba for its good weather and great defenses. His villa was a rather lavish mansion, originally built by the Medici family. Besides that, he had another summer residence, also opulently furnished and fitted for parties and visitors."

"Wasn't he guarded well?" I asked.

"A British officer, Neil Campbell, was his jailor."

"So, Napoleon was not really alone?" I continued my inquiry.

"No, and, although his second wife, Marie Louise, refused to join him in exile, his mistress, the Polish countess, Maria Walenska, joined him in greatest secrecy."

"And what of his first wife, Josephine?" I inquired further.

"Oh, the marriage was annulled because she had no children with him. But somewhat hypocritically, he wrote a last letter to her, saying 'Never forget him who has never forgotten you and will never ever forget you.'"

I could not restrain myself. "He was a liar and a hypocrite, and he treated women shamefully."

"Yes," replied Mycroft. "And he once said 'If you wish to be a success in this world, promise everything, deliver nothing!'"

"He was a devil!" pronounced Dr. Watson.

"And outrageously conceited," echoed Mycroft. "It is reported that in a letter, he wrote that he never doubted he was wise enough to teach law to lawyers, science to scientists, and religion to popes!"

"How absurd," I said, indignantly. "The man was surely a self-deluded villain. But how did he escape from Elba so easily?"

"Now that is a fascinating story!" said Mycroft, leaning forward in his chair.

"I heard from my many contacts in the government that Napoleon learned about the plans of the British to relocate him to the desolate island of St. Helena. This did not suit his plans at all. He would be far from his native France, where his supporters had begun activities to dethrone Louis XVIII and return Napoleon to power."

"And that's when he decided to escape?" I ventured.

"He consulted with his mother, who had stayed on the island with him. Her advice: 'Go my son … fulfill your destiny.'"

I interrupted. "Was ever a mother's love so misplaced!"

"Well," continued Mycroft, by now accustomed to the many interruptions, "when Neil Campbell, his guardian and jailor left for England to give reports on Napoleon, the sly emperor saw his chance to escape. In a daring move, Napoleon hastily assembled a small fleet of ships, disguised as British vessels, and with an army of loyal companions left the island with no resistance. Now, among those on board was a certain Count d'Montalon, who falsely professed loyalty to the emperor."

"Amazing," mused Dr. Watson. "The fox had flown the coop!"

Mycroft emphasized. "And Napoleon had even met with officials on Elba to tell them he planned to leave!"

"What gall!" I remarked.

"The bold prison break worked!" uttered Mycroft. "The French were taken off guard, the English not able to act quickly or effectively, and Napoleon's supporters were jubilant. He arrived as a hero in France. Only Napoleon would have pulled off that escape!"

Watson spoke up. "But we showed him just a little later, at the Battle of Waterloo. Napoleon was forced to abdicate for a second and final time!"

Now, Dr. Watson took over the story, adding his contribution to the fascinating tale.

"Napoleon thought he would escape to America, trying to wiggle out of his punishment, like the slippery eel that he was. But the Royal Navy sent a ship-of-the-line, to foil his plans."

"Yes, Doctor," added Mycroft. "Then he had the gall to surrender to Britain, where he hoped to receive an estate in Great Britain, on which he could retire."

"The nerve of that man," I remarked. "He had no repentance!"

"Well," pronounced Mycroft, "there was no chance that our government would allow such a dastardly person to live in our midst! We needed somewhere secure and distant from European activities."

"And the desolate island of St. Helena was the very place," said Watson, with satisfaction. "We did not want a second escape this time!"

Mycroft added, "And so, this time the British government would spend 8 million pounds a year for a fleet of ships and 5,000 soldiers to make sure that 'the fox' didn't escape. The once mighty general had no one to rule, and no more wars to fight."

"He was a fish out of water," commented Dr. Watson.

"More like a beached whale," corrected Mycroft.

"He was lodged in Longwood House, a large island dwelling that was cold, drafty, and infested with rats!"

I could not restrain myself. "Fitting companions for his royal majesty!"

"Thus, before long, his health started to decline," said Mycroft, seeming to bring an end to his tale.

"Napoleon is reputed to have said: 'to die is nothing, but to live defeated and without glory is to die every day!'"

Mycroft lowered his voice, as if to divulge a great secret. "It was decided, at the highest levels of British Intelligence, that someone had to undertake the mission to end Napoleon's life."

Dr. Watson and Mrs. Hudson looked at each other in surprise.

"It was both dangerous and delicate, for it had to look as if it was the result of natural causes. We did not want him to appear a martyr. The legend of Napoleon, already building in France, might rekindle a resurgence of French militancy. A secret delegation was sent to contact the one man who could best handle the job, none other than Count d'Montalon! Yes, the same count who had helped the escape from Elba would now plan his death."

Mycroft's face lit up with a sense of satisfaction. "What a delicious irony. D'Montalon was promised wealth beyond his wildest dreams. He was heavily in debt due to his incessant gambling and taste for the high life. Of course, we had planned to denounce him and be rid of him permanently after the deed was done. The disgusting man, who was rumored to have stolen money from his own regiment and even killed his own brother, agreed to the task and was sent to St. Helena to gain the old emperor's trust."

Dr. Watson delighted in the irony of the situation. "Who better to kill a viper than another viper?"

"So, Count d'Montalon again became a confidant of Napoleon and served his pastry and brandy at evening meals. It was during those festive occasions when the deluded emperor began writing his memoirs, and the count used his skill with poisons to deliver daily doses of charm and arsenic to his unsuspecting companion. Napoleon Bonaparte would never threaten the British Empire again."

Mycroft was now speaking excitedly. "The little emperor's last days were filled with pain as the poison took effect. In those last days, d'Montalon persuaded Napoleon to make him the beneficiary of his will, to the amount of over two million francs. As he lay dying, Napoleon told d'Montalon that he had hidden a vast treasure to be used to finance his return from exile again. The treasure, spoils of war from his many campaigns in foreign lands, included a great number of precious jewels. Instead, he ended up a bitter and disillusioned man."

Dr. Watson slammed his fist down on the arm of his chair. "Thus, ever the fate of all tyrants."

"It would seem so," said Mycroft. Then he went on with his story. "Napoleon made the captain swear that he would use the money to finance schemes that could lead to the eventual downfall of his great enemy … the British Empire. If he could not have his victory militarily, he would have his revenge economically. D'Montalon swore falsely that he would do so, but when the old emperor died, he found the treasure and kept it for himself.

"Now the British Government sent an agent to kill their assassin, but having suspected their intent all along, (the criminal mind trusts no one), he quickly hid the treasure on the deserted island of Tristan da Cunha, located about 1300 miles to the northeast of the island of St. Helena. The island is considered to be the most remote settlement on earth! Then setting sail for South America, he disappeared into the jungles."

Doctor Watson was overwhelmed. "Is that where you came into the story, Mycroft?"

"Exactly right, Doctor. I was privy to the affair because of my position as consultant and advisor to Parliament on British finances. It was my duty … nay, my privilege … to hunt down clues leading to the recovery of the treasure in the interests of the Crown. Its value could be applied to the tremendous cost of the Napoleonic Wars that had nearly bankrupted our government."

"Yes, I've read that part of the defeat of Napoleon was due to the economic power of the banking house of the Rothschilds," Dr. Watson added in an effort to show some comprehension of the matter.

"Precisely, Dr. Watson. Their financial aid made them very wealthy heroes."

Dr. Watson and I were fascinated by Mycroft's story of the Rothschilds. He told how they had made their initial fortune during the French Revolution, and then by lending funds to the British when they were at war with the American colonies. Finally, when Napoleon's armies were ravaging Europe, the Rothschilds lent money to the British government to pay for troops and armaments.

Then Mycroft sat up straight in his chair.

"Money talks! … and most loudly when hot-tempered princes are at war with each other, for victory equals power! One of the Rothschilds once said, 'If I control a country's finances, I care not who makes its laws!'

"But their public image was tarnished by rumors of unsavory contacts and sinister affairs. We have always suspected that they became involved with Count d'Montalon in some nefarious economic schemes and suffered from the association. The count, of course, only increased his power to undermine the British system."

"And the fate of this count?" prompted Dr. Watson.

"D'Montalon was declared traitor to the Empire and subject to the death penalty. Some years passed, but he was never caught. He had gathered a band of thugs around him and trained them in his evil craft. But as luck would have it, he contracted a rare jungle fever, from which, thankfully, he did not recover. While he lay dying, he told his most trusted companion in crime, whom he had come to think of as a son, the whereabouts of the treasure. He made him swear an oath to use it to bring ruin upon the British Empire. Oddly enough, the young man, a certain Moriarty by name, was to stay true to the oath he had given to his mentor in crime."

Doctor Watson jumped up from his chair. "Moriarty? The same…"

"Yes, Doctor, the same evil Moriarty that Sherlock eventually set out to destroy. After this incident, my brother dubbed him 'The Napoleon of Crime,' after his original benefactor. For my taste, it was a rather overly romanticized nom de guerre, but then I always thought my younger brother had a certain unrestrained panache about him."

Poor Doctor Watson could not contain himself. "Yes, yes, but the treasure. What about the treasure?"

"Well, as I have said, all this was told to bring my brother up to date concerning the history of the case. Of course, Sherlock had heard rumors of the legend of the emperor's fabulous treasure and, through his own sources, he learned that Trayer and Moriarty were connected with Count d'Montalon's treasure scheme, and were somewhere in this section of London. That is why he sought lodgings at Mrs. Hudson's establishment."

In a flash of recognition, I interrupted again. "Now I understand why Mr. Holmes was so persistent to obtain a room in my house. And he must have sensed that Mrs. Warren was referring to Trayer when she hysterically interrupted our first meeting."

"Yes, yes, Mrs. Hudson, but our immediate problem was to find the treasure. Sherlock and I deduced that it must have been nearby, because Moriarty and his thugs had come out in the open to get it from Trayer. The man could not be forced to divulge his secret and so he suffered that terrible death at the hands of those villains.

"As Sherlock and I looked around the room for clues, I remembered saying to him to take care not to get too close to the tank, for those deadly fish were still hungry. The deadly piranhas were placidly swimming in the tank, completely ignoring the skeletal hand sitting on the bottom, which they had attacked during their feeding frenzy.

"My brother tried to respond with his usual offhanded analytic detachment. 'The King Emperor Piranha, Pygocentrun piraya, normally found in the Amazonian River systems.'

"I persisted. 'Yes,' responded Sherlock, 'but now they're here in London, biting off peoples' hands!' We both stared at the bones of the severed hand in the tank. The hideous sight seemed to compel our attention, almost hypnotically.

"Sherlock was frustrated and furious. 'I feel like a blind man groping in the dark. We must be overlooking the obvious, some piece of evidence that will lift the veil from our eyes.'

"Sensing that his recent brush with death had left him somewhat shaken, I challenged him. 'Sherlock, are we not brothers? Do we not share that power of intuition that sets us apart from the multitude? Two peas in the same pod, as it were. We have disciplined ourselves to seek that particular truth, which, above all, leads to the unraveling of the mystery.'

"Sherlock just stared at me, the way he often did when I was lecturing him as a boy. Then he responded with grim intensity, as I knew he would. 'Yes, Mycroft, we are at the very door of the solution to our puzzle. Now we must find the right key.'

"I reminded him that father used to say that the hardest things to recognize are those that lay before our very eyes.

"He nodded. 'Yes, the eyes are frequently fooled into overlooking the obvious, being deceived by the trivial.'

"Then staring at the severed hand in the tank, I made an off-handed remark to Sherlock. 'I don't know what is more hypnotic, the sight of that severed hand or the sparkling gravel beneath those creatures.'

"Sherlock recalled the dying man's screams. 'Sentinels at the gate', that's what he called them. Why the fascination with these vicious pets? These King Emperors! Emperors! Could they be protecting something?'

" 'What do you mean, brother?' asked Sherlock. "His remark set me thinking.

"His eyes opened widely; a flash of insight glowed within. 'Mycroft, we may have found our needle in a haystack, our key as it were to the door!'

" 'Or in this case', mused Sherlock, 'a key to the treasure box in the protective custody of these fiercely dedicated sentinels. The sentinels at the gate.'

"We cautiously inspected the gruesome scene and, sure enough, the gravel in the tank had been disturbed by the ravenous fish, exposing areas of uncharacteristic splendor. Trayer had found the perfect hiding place for the old emperor's treasure. It was there, under the gravel, guarded by the best possible sentries … the vicious King Emperor Piranhas. Now how to separate the treasure from the tenacious guardians?

" 'Don't go off all emotional', I said to my younger brother, 'we don't want a second severed hand as a companion to the first.' But it was no use warning Sherlock about danger. It only made him more determined.

" 'Mycroft, may I borrow your walking stick?' He said it so innocently that I foolishly handed it to him. Then, he dipped it into the tank and let the vicious creatures clamp onto the end of it with their razor-like teeth. Then, one by one, he flipped them off into a chamber pot with all the abandonment of a young lad gone fishing. Imagine that! Going fishing with my favorite walking stick! Only my younger brother would come up with so ingenious a way of emptying the tank. When the deed was done, he seemed rather proud of his accomplishment. Then he simply returned my all-but-destroyed stick to me with a 'Thank you, brother.' Even as a boy Sherlock was always ruining something or other of mine. But I guess that's what younger brothers do. Positively irritating."

"I notice that you still carry the same walking stick with you today," I said trying to hide a smirk.

"Oh, yes, well it still has some functional value, you know."

"And possibly some sentimental value?" added Dr. Watson.

"Nothing of the kind, Doctor. Now, where was I? Oh yes, the next step was to carry that heavy tank over to the bathtub down the hallway. It was quite a task, but Sherlock was renowned for his strength as a young man and never ceased to find an opportunity to show it. He did have a flair for the eccentric, which, I must say, never diminished with age. I, on the other hand, have always been possessed of a quieter variety of bravado.

"Then Sherlock and I spilled the contents of the tank into the bathtub, being careful to cover the drain. One by one, we proceeded to separate the glittering gems from the baser sediment. It was like Christmas ... diamonds, emeralds, rubies, pearls ... a fortune to be sure! Trayer had recovered the treasure and brought it back to London, hoping to use it to finance his retirement in opulent splendor."

Doctor Watson settled into his chair with great satisfaction. "And so, the Holmes brothers recovered the wealth that helped Britain to gain her proper place as the overseer of the Pax Britannica. The treasure was passed from Napoleon, to Count d'Montalon, to Moriarty and Trayer, then intercepted by Sherlock and Mycroft Holmes before it could be sold to the Rothschilds, its probable intended destination. The world was set right again. What a remarkable story. Why this is just the very thing to write about, a fitting tribute to British crime detection. And I shall call it *The Adventure of the Napoleon Treasure*. It will surely be a great hit with the public."

Mycroft settled a cold eye on the doctor. "I'm afraid not, Doctor Watson. This whole affair is too delicate a matter to be let out to the public. Our diplomatic position would be compromised if it were generally known that we had clandestinely seized a French national treasure as spoils of war. No! No! Sherlock wisely decided to keep the whole matter hush, hush!"

Doctor Watson could not control his disappointment. "And so, Holmes' most significant case is to be buried forever!"

I had been listening patiently to Mycroft and Doctor Watson, but now I felt I had to speak up. "Dear Doctor, it is a secret that I have kept ever since that first meeting with Mr. Holmes, so long ago. That intimate bond has united us as confidants and, yes, even as friends, all these years. I would not spoil his memory for anything."

"You knew about the diplomatic incident and the treasure of Napoleon?" asked Dr. Watson, completely caught off-guard at her pronouncement.

"Gentlemen, I must tell you that many things were held in confidence between Mr. Holmes and me. It comforted me that he thought enough to share some of his most interesting cases with me. Of course, I was sworn to secrecy, and have always kept my silence about the details of his cases. In fact, Dr. Watson, it is you who have exposed many of his adventures!"

"Why, yes, but always with his permission," said Dr. Watson, defensively.

"Of course, and so I have kept the sanctity of a priest's confessional about Mr. Holmes' affairs. In certain times, when the oppression of the world came down heavily on him, I was his confidant. Like the son I never had, he fulfilled my need for intimate sharing that every mother desires. I like to think it sometimes relieved him of his need for the cocaine solution, which I prayed he would abandon. But we will speak no more of secret affairs, and instead enjoy the shared bond between us."

Doctor Watson smiled approvingly. "Just so. It must remain the shared bond that unites us all."

Then, raising his glass, which I must admit he had refilled quite a few times during the evening, he proposed a toast. "Christmas is a time of remembering; of stirring up the embers that feed the flames of memory and keep alive the images that warm our hearts. It is in this spirit that we recall an earlier time, when life seemed simpler, happier and kinder to our dreams."

Mycroft cringed impatiently. "Oh, Doctor Watson, please do get on with it, else we shall be toasting here 'til next Christmas."

Then preempting the Doctor's eloquence, I raised my glass, and put forth a simple statement. "To Sherlock Holmes. To his memory and his legacy. May it live forever."

The glasses came together with a ringing that matched the church bells sounding in the streets below.

"Here! Here! A Happy Christmas to all."

Addendum

It should be noted that Mrs. Hudson's account of Sherlock Holmes' first important case, was confided to Dr. Watson and Mycroft Holmes, at Christmas time when the great detective was in seclusion, after the struggle at Reichenbach Falls. Dr. Watson had written of it in The Final Problem. However, Holmes eventually returned in the case of The Empty Room, when he met Colonel Sebastian Moran.

In our story, when Mrs. Hudson meets with Dr. Watson and Mycroft Holmes, the trio piece together the fascinating story of Holmes' first significant case. Dr. Watson, eager to publish it called it The Adventure of the Napoleon Treasure. However, Mycroft cautioned. "Our diplomatic position would be compromised if it were generally known that we had clandestinely seized a French National Treasure as spoils of war." And so, Sherlock Holmes' most significant case was buried forever!

ADVENTURE No. 3
The Gladstone Kidnapping

THE GLADSTONE KIDNAPPING

In my time, I have had the fortune to meet some of the most influential people of my age ... scientists, philosophers, leaders of countries and, at the darker end of the human spectrum, the misfortune to encounter terrorists, assassins, master criminals, and black-mailers! However, the Case of the Gladstone Kidnapping plunged me into circumstances that nearly ended my life and the lives of a family of friends, including a special little girl named Natalie.

We were approaching the 1900's, a new and exciting era, and I was approaching my thirty-third year on earth ... my birthday! When one considers the age of the earth and, indeed the age of our universe, a man's life is but a brief, insignificant, momentary flash of time by comparison. Yet, within that flash are contained events so full of meaning that we absurdly mark them by the elaborate ritual of a birthday!

Dr. Watson and Mrs. Hudson had insisted that we celebrate both events this year by having a small celebration to which a few friends had been invited. At the dining room table, cluttered with a collection of culinary delights, Mrs. Hudson had placed a three-layered cake decorated with one big candle. Dr. Watson rose to his feet and proposed a toast.

"As we approach the new century, a time of expansion of the human mind and the technology resulting from it, I give you, Sherlock Holmes... friend and colleague ..."

Getting into the festive spirit, my brother, Mycroft, interrupted the doctor with an unexpected embellishment, "... and one of the greatest minds of this or any other century, past or present."

Everyone laughed and drank to my health.

Mrs. Hudson spoke up. "And best wishes for a celebration free of crime!"

"If crime ever does take a holiday!" I cynically added.

"Please, Mr. Holmes, don't spoil it! All is right with the world!" Mrs. Hudson added as she lit the candle on the cake.

But all was not right with the world. There came an impatient knock at the door, bringing our festivities to a halt.

"Now who could that be?" asked Mrs. Hudson, as she went to the door and opened it.

There in the doorway stood a large and somber figure of a man dressed in uniform.

"Important message for Sherlock Holmes," he said stepping aggressively into the room.

I arose from my place at the table and answered, "I'm Sherlock Holmes, come in and deliver your message!"

The man walked over to me and handed me the message. The envelope was marked with a government seal. I opened it nervously and read it quickly.

"A summons to Number 10 Downing Street!" I said in surprise. "This must be urgent."

"Yes, it is," said the messenger. "You must come at once! It's a matter of life and death."

I turned to Mrs. Hudson.

"Mrs. Hudson would you be my hostess in proxy and continue the party in my name?"

I felt I had just received my birthday wish ... a brand-new case to solve!

Everyone offered their good wishes and I hurried off with Dr. Watson and brother Mycroft at my side.

"I'll save a piece of birthday cake for each of you!" Mrs. Hudson said as we left.

As we got into the coach, I was eager for our departure. The adventure had begun and I mumbled under my breath, "The game's afoot!" as we sped off.

The coach rumbled along as it turned onto Downing Street, and headed to the building at the far end. Number 10 Downing Street was a large structure, originally three properties, which had been consolidated in 1684 by Sir George Downing, into a three-story building, with attic and basement.

As the coach pulled up to the entrance, the distinctive Georgian-style door came into view. It was a small, six-paneled door, made of black oak and surrounded by a cream-colored casing, adorned with a semicircular fanlight window. Painted in white between the top and middle sets of panels, appeared the number '10'. A black iron knocker in the shape of a lion's head sat between the two middle panels.

The messenger walked over to the door and sounded the lion's head knocker.

"Important guests to see the Prime Minister," he announced to the guard, who had opened the door and stepped outside.

We were escorted through the doorway and into the entrance hall. Black and white marble tiles covered the entrance floor.

Off the entrance hall were three interlinked state drawing rooms: The Pillared Drawing Room (so named because of its twin Ionic pilasters with straight pediments at one end); The Terra Cotta Drawing Room (the middle of the three rooms); and the White Drawing room (used for private meetings).

"This way, gentlemen," said the guide.

We were led into the Pillared Drawing Room, the largest and most splendid of the rooms.

"Wait here. The Prime Minister will be with you in a moment," were the instructions.

Impatiently, we awaited the arrival of the Prime Minister.

We noticed that over the fireplace hung the portraits of Queen Elizabeth I, and Prime Minister William Pitt. The magnificence of the room was enhanced by a 16th century Persian carpet that covered almost the entire floor.

Hurried footsteps announced the arrival of our prominent host.

"Good afternoon, gentlemen!"

There before us stood William E. Gladstone, regarded as the greatest statesman of his day.

"Hello, Prime Minister, we are here at your bidding."

"Yes, yes, thank you for coming!"

The strain of office was apparent from his shuffling gate, and the bowed stature of his body. He had unquestionably become an old man. Hair, white and entangled, crowned his now unkempt and disheveled appearance. The once resonant voice had lost its forceful eloquence, and a desire to be released from the burdens of office was painfully apparent. The emotional stress resulting from the contentious events in Parliament seemed to have led to an inevitable breakdown in his strength. The stately, arrogant façade that had formerly characterized his public persona was now replaced by an aging, humbled, saddened, shell of a man.

"I could choose no others for this dangerous mission, my friends. Your reputations precede you and your brother, Mycroft, whom I know so well from his many services to us in the past. And this other gentleman?"

"He is Dr. Watson, my dear friend and colleague. He was of late a surgeon in our British Armed Forces," I said proudly.

The Prime Minister brought us to a small private conference room, adjacent to the large drawing room.

"Gentlemen, I fear that we have a very serious and very dangerous situation on our hands!" he said, his eyes starting to glaze over with tears.

"My daughter, Lady Mary Gladstone Drew and her husband, my son-in-law, Sir Harry Drew have been kidnapped! With them was my granddaughter, Natalie, their daughter. I expect that a king's ransom will be demanded for their return. Our enemies will use it to finance their corrupt schemes to cripple our government. They know that I would do anything to ensure their safe return."

"Have you received a ransom note?" I asked.

"Not yet," replied the Prime Minister, "but I expect one soon."

Mycroft spoke up. "We must apprehend the villain before his plan is fully executed. And we must stop him before news of the kidnapping gets out. Otherwise, this may set a precedent for extortion by kidnapping other members of the government."

"Do we know who is behind this treacherous deed?" asked the Prime Minister.

"I don't know for sure yet, but I suspect my arch-enemy, Professor James Moriarty. Only he would be so bold and would have the criminal resources to threaten the families of high government officials!" I speculated.

"And my greatest fear is that he would not leave any witnesses left alive!" said Dr. Watson.

"You mean he would kill my family?" said the Prime Minister, fearing the worst!

"You never can tell what's in the mind of that fiendish criminal!" I answered. "Now let's discuss the strategy of handling this affair."

The Prime Minister interrupted the conversation for a moment.

"Gentlemen, I must tell you a secret about my granddaughter, Natalie." His face turned quite pale and stressed.

"Natalie has a delicate constitution! It is not generally known out-side the family circles. But her condition makes the dilemma even more serious. We have found that maintaining rigorous hygiene precautions, and spending considerable amounts of time in the fresh air and sunshine are very beneficial for her. If she does not stick to these regimens, her health might decline rapidly. The stress of the kidnapping may also bring disastrous consequences.

"To me, Natalie is like a fragile flower, to be ever cared for and pro-tected."

There was no doubting the depth of his love for his granddaughter.

"I understand, Prime Minister. Now tell me what do you know of the kidnapping?"

"Well, some progress has been made," he confided. "So far, Her Maj-esty's Intelligence Service has gathered information indicating that the kidnappers have taken them from London to Calais and Paris, by means of the Orient Express. Then they transferred to the Arlberg Railway line and on to Zurich, Switzerland!"

"Switzerland!" said Watson astonished.

"Yes," the Prime Minister continued. "Then the train eventually cuts through Liechtenstein. It appears that they stopped at the deserted Gutenberg Castle, where, no doubt, they are holding their quarry and planning their next move."

"Then there is no time to lose," I said.

Dr. Watson, Mycroft and I speedily set off for the next train from London, with a 'God speed' from the Prime Minister. In truth, the trip was rather lengthy and when we reached the Arlberg Railway line, the cramped seats were just too much for my long legs. I decided to take a stroll out on the platform that connected our car with the next. As I stepped into the platform, I became aware of a dark figure just behind me. A terrible fear came over me … could we have been followed?

I turned to see who it was, but before I could completely view my unknown visitor, I felt a violent push. Suddenly, I was headed out of the train into the cold air outside. I instinctively grabbed for anything to cling to, but all I could grasp was the bottom of the window sill, just a few inches away. I heard a hideous laugh and then …

"Goodbye, Mr. Holmes. Happy Birthday!"

The thought of Moriarty flashed into my mind, but I had no time to identify my assailment accurately. I was clutching desperately to the thinnest of edging beneath the window. I held on tightly, but as the train rattled on, I could feel my fingers losing their grip!

At that instant, the train whistle blew, indicating that we were crossing a narrow bridge over a deep river. I peered over my shoulder to see the lay of the land below. Fortunately, the river was directly below me, possibly a 200-foot drop. I feared that I could hold on no longer, but if I could manage to drop down straight into the water, it might break my fall. It was my only chance … I let go, pushing outward to clear the bridge!

As I began my plunge into hell, I thought I heard someone call out to me, "Holmes! Holmes!"

Down, down, down, I plunged into the churning water. I struggled to loosen my cape and hat, so as not to be dragged down by their weight when I hit the water. What was actually only a matter of seconds, seemed like an eternity. Upon entering the water at top speed, I held my breath while fighting the inertia of the fall. *Splash!* I plunged deep into the freezing water. Then I swam for the surface with all the strength I could summon.

Finally reaching the surface, my lungs gasping for air, I was immediately caught up in the swift current pulling me downstream. It was my good fortune that a large tree branch came floating by me. I grabbed it and held on for dear life, as the rapids beat against me.

Managing to steer toward the shore, I reached up and caught hold of a sagging tree branch at the shoreline. I hung there for a while to regain my wits, and finally lifted my weight out of the water. Hand over hand, I maneuvered myself onto the shore, where I lay exhausted for nearly twenty minutes.

Finally, I regained enough strength to traverse a pathway leading to a clearing that eventually connected to a road inland. I made my way up an alpine slope and found what I thought appeared to be a deserted cabin. With any luck, I thought, I would find some way to treat my cuts and bruises. I stumbled to the door, and to my surprise, an old man opened it.

"Could you help a traveler in need?" were the first words out of my mouth.

The old man smiled. "Gladly. Come in and rest yourself," was the reply.

I crawled into the cabin and sat down on a rustic old chair.

"It looks like you've had a rough trip!" said the old man.

"Yes, I'm on a journey to Liechtenstein," I answered.

"Well, you're in luck! I am very familiar with the way there and I can even show you some shortcuts, if you'll allow me to accompany you!"

"I would be grateful if it's not too inconvenient!"

"Not at all," he smiled.

He said the words so sincerely that I instantly decided to follow his lead. It was all too good to be true, I thought.

After I rested for a while, I regained some of my strength. Then we decided to set out on our trip.

I inquired how he came to know so much about the alpine countryside.

"Well," he began, "I was raised in these mountains and know them like the back of my hand. As a boy, my father showed me the secret pass that Hannibal used to march his army across the Alps during his invasion of Italy, in the ancient days. It can lead us to Zurich and from there to Liechtenstein."

I was overjoyed and had no reason to doubt my benefactor's account.

Soon we were making our way up the long path that would bring me to my destination. It took several hours to clear the Alps and get into the low lands where the path was more easily traversed. In a few more hours, we reached Liechtenstein.

Inquiring at the train station in town, we were told that two rough-looking men had gotten off here with a lady, a gentleman, and a little girl. It was suggested that they were headed for Gutenberg Castle to rest for a while.

"I know the castle," said the old man. "I'll be happy to show you the way!"

We eventually reached the castle. It was situated on a high hill, surrounded by dense vegetation on all sides.

The old man seemed curious about my intentions.

"What is your business here?"

I hesitated to tell him my true reasons, so I made up a story.

"This is the birthplace of my grandfather and I have come all this way to see the place of my ancestors."

The old man seemed to accept my story, and so we proceeded through the brush and reached the large entrance door of the castle.

"Now we must enter carefully," I warned.

"How so? The castle should be deserted!" answered the old man.

"Yes, but it doesn't hurt to be careful," I insisted.

Then the words came that made my heart sink.

"Too late, Mr. Holmes, you have fallen into my trap!"

The old man raised his hunting gun, which he said he had brought along for safety. He pointed it straight at me.

"Caught in the trap, just like an animal, you see!" He laughed and whistled a signal. Out of the castle came Moriarty and a large, brutish man, brandishing a pistol.

"Welcome, Mr. Holmes. We were expecting you to show up sometime!" taunted my mortal enemy.

"You see, we stationed old Vossler at the cabin in the event that you survived the train 'accident'. His story of being raised in the Alps was a cunning fabrication to lull you into a false sense of security. In fact, it was part of my master plan to cover all the eventualities of a rescue attempt. You see, a number of cabins were occupied to trick you, whichever route you took. And you suspected nothing! Shame … Mr. Holmes!"

The words stung, but I remained silent. I was amazed that Moriarty's web of evil extended far beyond the streets of London … even to the European continent and perhaps beyond!

Moriarty spoke again.

"Please accept our invitation to old Gutenberg Castle."

We entered and found ourselves in a large deserted Great Hall, dimly lit. As my eyes became accustomed to the darkness, I saw three figures bound securely to wooden chairs that were part of the sparse furnishings of the medieval castle.

I greeted the prisoners. "Lord and Lady Drew and my lovely young lady, Natalie, I'm Sherlock Holmes, sent by your father, the Prime Minister. I'm sorry for the predicament I find you in."

"I wish we could have met under better circumstances, Mr. Holmes," said Lord Drew.

"Amen to that," I answered.

Natalie spoke up. "Oh, Mr. Holmes, I've heard so much about you ... and to finally meet you ...I'm thrilled!"

I addressed the delightful young lady, "I wish I could help you get better treatment than this!" I said smiling at the innocent exuberance of such a fine member of the Gladstone family.

"That's our Natalie, a joy to us all," said Lady Drew.

Moriarty interrupted, wishing to stifle our brief, pleasant exchange.

"Well, Mr. Holmes, your rescue attempt was not very successful. And, finally, I will be rid of my last impediment to world power."

"Moriarty, you are sick with power!" I yelled out.

"Well, that's an ailment you'll never cure me of, Mr. Holmes."

Natalie scolded, "You're a terrible man and you should be put in jail, Mr. Moriarty!"

"But it is you who are in jail, little lady ... my jail!" said Moriarty with an evil smile.

Then I was tied up securely and thrown onto the floor in a dark corner of the hall, there being no other furniture left in the room. Moriarty and his henchmen walked some distance away, discussing what to do with us.

At that moment, a rat ran across the floor in front of me. It paused to survey my predicament and then ran off into a large hole in the wall just beyond me.

Moriarty saw the rat and found it amusing. "Sherlock Holmes, this is your fate, then ... tied up like a rat caught in a trap. What a pitiful end to your illustrious career!"

Then Moriarty instructed old Vossler and the other man.

"After I leave to take care of the rest of this business, just kill them and be rid of them. I must bargain with the Prime Minister to increase the power of my organization. Once I have the money, it won't matter what happens to our prisoners."

Then he left. The two men remained behind to complete their task.

Then, the two men tossed a coin to see who would kill whom. Old Vossler won the toss to end my life. He walked over and pointed his hunting rifle at me.

"Nothing personal. It's just a job. Goodbye, Mr. Sherlock Holmes," were his final words.

Bang! Bang! Two shots rang out.

But it was our captors who fell to the floor … dead!

Then a familiar voice rang out, "Holmes, are you all, right?"

It was Watson, closely followed by Mycroft!

"Watson, Mycroft, just in the nick of time," I cried out. "Ever my faithful benefactors and constant protectors, you haven't failed me!"

"Rather my life than yours, Holmes," answered Watson.

"My sentiments, also," echoed Mycroft.

Watson and Mycroft then released us from our bonds. I introduced them to the Drew family. Natalie was particularly impressed with Dr. Watson.

"But Watson, how did you find us? I thought it was all over for us all!"

"I thought you were never to be seen again!" said Watson. "When I saw you clinging to the window outside the train, I called to you. Holmes! Holmes! … Then you were gone … swallowed up by the raging water below."

"We thought we had lost you, forever!" added Mycroft.

Watson continued. "I rushed to the front car to inform the engineer of the tragedy that had just occurred. When I got there, he was unaware of the drama that had just unfolded minutes before."

"You must stop the train," I demanded. "There has been a terrible accident. My friend has fallen into the river below. Please stop the train!"

The engineer stared at me in disbelief and then uttered the most tragic words I had ever heard. "Hopeless, it's just hopeless!"

"What do you mean?" I insisted.

"No man could ever survive the fall … its 200 feet down to the river and then the swift current would swallow him up!" came the answer.

"The train moved on. I stood there confused and consumed with grief."

"But how in the world did you two find me?" I asked.

"Well," said Watson, "I refused to believe that you had died. I could not conceive of a world without you!"

Mycroft interrupted. "Back tracking! We decided to track your travels from Liechtenstein."

Watson eagerly jumped into the conversation.

"Yes, we inquired at the train station and learned that an old man with a hunting gun and a younger man, with a disheveled appearance, had inquired about Gutenberg Castle. It seemed a logical place for a rendez-vous, so we made our way there, being careful to hide our presence, in the event that our enemies had arrived before us."

Mycroft continued the story. "We saw you being taken into the castle and waited for the proper moment to make our presence known."

I then remarked, "No question about it. The two gun shots seem appropriate enough to announce your arrival!"

"But it is all over now, Holmes, and you're here, safe and sound!"

And so, the adventure was over. And I thought to myself, "What is an adventure but, an inconvenience taken in the right spirit!"

We wasted no time to take the return train back to London. Needless to say, the reunion was a joyous one. The Prime Minister greeted us all with happiness and relief.

"Grandfather! Grandfather!" shouted Natalie, running up and giving him a big hug.

His eyes brightened and his lips opened up with a large grateful smile. I could hardly believe that such a tiny figure could bring so much joy to his countenance. It struck me how the power of the love of a child could work wonders to heal the human spirit.

I have the feeling when she grows up, she will be a powerful force in British society.

"Natalie! Natalie! Natalie! We have been so worried about you and your parents," he said embracing his beloved granddaughter.

"No need to worry, Grandfather. We were safe with Mr. Holmes," she answered with the trusting assurance of an innocent child.

I stepped forward.

"Prime Minister, we have returned your family, safe and sound."

The Prime Minister summoned all his dignity and responded cordially, "Gentlemen, I thank you for your help when our country was in need! I am in your debt. Ask what you will!"

I responded, "We ask only that you will allow us to take up your cause and set things right!"

So, the threat to English government had been averted, Moriarty's plot to extort ransom from the British state thwarted, and the Prime Minister's family had been saved from disaster.

After the events of the Gladstone kidnapping, we settled back down to the safety and security of life under the British crown. A façade of protection set in. But, not for long. With Moriarty at large to hatch more evil plots, I had to be constantly on guard, for he had escaped to somewhere in Europe, relying on his many connections to secure his anonymity. The spider was free to spin his web of chaos once more!

After a time, I lost touch with Natalie, for her life's path was quite different from mine. Then, one day, fate brought us together again. It was May 19, 1898. I can't forget the day the great, old man, Gladstone, died.

A host of admirers and well-wishers gathered at Westminster Abbey to pay tribute to the Prime Minister, who had been the man of his age.

As the bells in the tower rang out in mournful tones, I felt compelled to survey the crowd to see who was present. All at once my eyes lighted on a pair of eyes that had first caught sight of mine. It was Natalie!

She was standing with her parents, but as soon as our eyes met, she quietly made her way through the crowd and, standing by my side, she took my hand in hers. It was the gentle hand of a young woman of thirteen, firmly grasping my rough, aging hand. Her sad eyes looked up to me.

"Grandfather is gone."

I nodded to her.

We stood there hand in hand until the services were concluded. Then she gave my hand a squeeze, let go, and slowly walked back to her parents. On the way, she hesitated as if to turn back for one final look. But she did not turn. Then she continued on to her parents' side.

The clouds above parted and the sun shone brightly. At that moment, I sensed that she had grown into a woman, ready to take her place in the British peerage and accept the responsibilities that would be expected of her. She would marry and become Lady Natalie, but to me she would always be the little princess, Natalie, the brightest star in my universe.

ADVENTURE NO. 4
The Hanged Man

Death in any form is not a pleasant sight.
But death by hanging is most gruesome.

THE HANGED MAN

There is something about returning to the memories of child-hood that presents a certain dreamlike quality to our recollections of the truth. The eyes of a child view things differently than the sharply focused vision of an adult. Yet time refocuses the lens of memory through which we see and remember, and sometimes robs us of our dreams, as reality intrudes.

Often the smallest scene or object can trigger a flood of memories that lay buried in the soul for many years … like an old picture taken from a forgotten drawer that stirs our mind's eye. Or like a simple carving of a favorite horse, called Palamedes, that I was holding in my hand, having just awakened from a deep sleep; it was a reminder of the gruesome death of my best boyhood friend, Matthew. I tried to put the memory out of my mind, but visions of the terrible event kept coming back to me.

"Holmes, are you awake?" The voice of another best friend, Watson, intruded on my daydreaming.

"Yes, Watson, did you sleep well?" I responded, trying to shake the drowsiness from my brain.

"Scotland Yard is calling for us … a strange case of murder and death in a bizarre setting. It's in your old neighborhood, in fact, where you grew up as a kid!"

We hurried to dress and gobbled down some breakfast.

"Off to our new adventure, Watson," I said, as I pulled on my cape and hat and rushed out of our flat.

I had mixed feelings about returning to my old neighborhood. I had not been there for many years, and I wondered how much it had changed.

We arrived just after the police. Inspector Lestrade came out to meet us.

"Holmes, Watson, thank you for coming to help us. Well, there it is … as hideous a sight as I have ever seen in all my days on the force. What do you say?"

Yes, it was hideous. There, decorating the branch of the old chestnut tree by the pond that I used to skate on, was a new and sickening sight. The figure of a man hanging from the longest branch covered with ice and snow presented a ghoulish spectacle. The slight wind imparted a force that set the frozen body in motion swinging to and fro, like some ridiculous pendulum of a bizarre clock.

"And see below," pointed out Lestrade. "The frozen body of a man caught in the act of trying to escape from his watery grave."

The fascinating tableau of death was so hypnotically compelling that I went over for a closer look.

"Who is the victim in the pond?" I managed to blurt out.

"Someone has identified him as a Mister Billy Blackwell, but the man hanging above remains a mystery," answered Lestrade.

"Billy Blackwell!" I remarked. "Yes, I remember him from my younger days."

"A notorious villain, who grew up in this neighborhood," remarked Lestrade, "a homegrown product of our own community!"

"Yes, a mean and vengeful criminal!" commented Watson.

As I stared at the scene, my mind was suddenly pulled back to the memory of my ninth birthday! The journey back brought me to a party given for the two of us … myself and my boyhood friend, Matthew.

We were born on the same day and we always celebrated twin birthdays. I was the son of a country squire, while he was the son of our stable groom. But status had no claim on our friendship. We had pledged that the bonds between us would never be broken. No two brothers were ever closer that the two of us.

Together, we blew out the candles on the cake, and everyone wished us a 'Happy Birthday'.

My mother asked, "What have you made for your birthday brother, Sherlock?"

That's when I pulled out the carving from my pocket. I had worked for months to carve the statue of our favorite horse, Palamedes.

"Here, Matthew, this is for you!"

Everyone clapped their approval.

"Thanks, Sherlock," he said, somewhat surprised. "I don't have as good a gift for you, I'm afraid."

He took the carving, feeling somewhat embarrassed.

"That's all right, Matt. Your friendship is the best gift I could ever want."

We embraced as two inseparable brothers.

The next day was cold and crisp … just the kind of day for having fun. We bundled up in several layers of clothing so we didn't mind the cold.

"Let's go to the old chestnut tree by the pond," suggested Matt.

"Last one there is a rotten egg!" I shouted.

We ran through the deep snow, slipping on the icy patches. Matt arrived first. He was very tall for his age and usually beat me in every race!

"Let's see who can climb to the highest branch," he challenged.

So we scrambled up to the very highest branch on the tree. I was good at climbing, so I reached the top before he did.

"King of the mountain!" I exclaimed, in triumph. "Father warned me not to climb trees in icy winter, but there's nothing to it!"

All of a sudden, true to my father's word, I lost my grip. "Matt, I'm slipping!"

"Hold on!" yelled Matt.

But it was no use. Down to the icy ground I fell!

Matthew called down to me, "Sherlock, did you hurt yourself?"

I tried to act bravely. "No, no, I'm just fine!"

But I wasn't fine … I felt a sharp pain in my right leg, and it hurt worse than ever when I tried to move it.

"I'll just rest here for a while," I said, trying not to show my distress.

Matt jumped down from the tree limb onto the icy pond.

Just then, a loud *Crack!* was heard. His weight was too much for the ice to hold. The ice began to splinter into pieces. Matt was being sucked down into an icy grave.

"Help!" he cried, reaching out to me.

But I was too far away and in too much pain to help.

Just then, some of the other neighborhood kids arrived. The oldest and biggest of the crowd was Billy Blackwell. He and his brothers, Jim and David, dominated the neighborhood. Also with the gang, was Billy's girlfriend, Barbara, a spoiled, selfish girl who was used to having her own way.

"Look at the clumsy boys," she mocked and laughed. "I wish I could have a picture of this!"

The other boys joined in and began to taunt us.

"How's the water, boys?"

I called out to them. "Help him someone, please help him!"

But they just laughed and watched him thrash about helplessly.

"I'm not getting wet just to help that silly boy!" said Barbara, cruelly.

Then they all turned and walked away laughing.

Meanwhile, Matt went down under the icy water and it didn't look as if he would be coming back up again.

I yelled at the top of my voice, "Help! Help! Help!"

I could not overcome my pain. I just watched helplessly, as my best friend grasped desperately for something to hold on to. But the more he reached out, the more the ice gave way around him. He was drowning and I could not help him!

Finally, my yelling had alerted some of the folk in the nearby manor house and they came running. Ironically, one of them was Matt's father, old Louis, and another was my father.

By now, Matt was nearly frozen stiff. He had stopped struggling. They pulled him out of the water and carried him back to the estate.

My father gave me a stern look and said, "You were warned not to climb that icy tree!"

I just looked down in shame and sorrow.

Matt was taken up to the master bedroom, where a warm fire was made in the nearby fireplace. His cold body was wrapped in warm blankets in hopes that we were not too late to save him. The doctor was sent for. When he arrived, he checked Matt's pulse. He shook his head and then turned to me.

"And now, let's attend to your leg, my boy!"

"Please don't worry about me. Just take care of Matthew!" I pleaded.

"We have done all that can be done for your friend. Now he is in the hands of the Lord!"

"Can't we do something else?" I asked.

He repeated, "All that can be done has been done. We will have to wait and see," he said, solemnly.

I cried.

For three days we kept vigil at Matthew's bed side. But each day he became worse than the day before. He developed pneumonia, which made his breathing difficult. Then, on the third day, he quietly slipped away. All our best efforts and prayers were in vain.

My best friend was no more, and I felt it was my fault entirely. I was given the carving of Palamedes, his birthday gift, as a keepsake for remembrance. I have kept it always and have never forgotten my brotherly comrade … Matthew.

I was called back to the present by a gentle nudge and the words, "Holmes, Holmes, the Inspector is speaking to you!"

"Yes, Inspector, what was that again?" I had regained my hold on the present.

"I said, what do you deduce from all this? Can you offer an explanation for this grizzly scene?"

"Well, I know enough about Billy to theorize that he was responsible for the hanging! Billy was a sadistic villain, who delighted in seeing his victims suffer. His vengeance carried far beyond death, even to the desecration of the body.

"I, myself, had dealings with him as a young boy. The journey back to that experience is one of my most horrible memories. But an autopsy should reveal much about the hanged man and his relationship to Billy."

"Quite so, Holmes. We'll set about taking him down from his macabre perch, and removing Billy Blackwell from his icy grave."

The hanged man was carefully lowered from the tree so as not to disturb any evidence on his body that might offer clues as to his identity and relationship to his murderer.

As for Billy Blackwell, the police began the delicate and dangerous task of removing him from his icy throne. As I looked at Billy's corpse, Dr. Watson, who had remained silent for most of this time, finally broke his silence.

"Are you all right, Holmes? You seem to be entranced in some painful childhood memories. Is there anything I can do to help?"

"The whole matter has brought back strong emotions that I thought were long buried … but I realize now that they were just waiting to surface, when provided with the proper trigger," I confessed.

"Look at Billy Blackwell, his frozen body with arms outstretched and eyes and mouth wide open, as if calling out for someone to help him … as my boyhood friend, Matthew, had done so many years ago. It is as if a drama of poetic justice is now being reenacted and finally played out to an audience of one … myself, Sherlock Holmes."

"Or, perhaps," observed Watson, "Billy Blackwell is acting out his final appeal for forgiveness to the creator above for all his sins!"

I was in no mood for forgiveness. "No amount of appeal can ever absolve his black heart!" I snarled. "He will surely be deposed to that dark place where all of his kind end up!"

The whole affair had touched me deeply, and I was surprised at my statement of condemnation. It wasn't kind, it wasn't charitable; it wasn't me … or was it? Who can tell the depths the human soul can descend to when hate overcomes the gentle façade of our good manners?

It took some time to extricate the two bodies from their frozen positions. Watson and I could only look on in disgust at the scene before us. One of the policemen was overcome by the ghastly condition of the bodies and fainted before he could even help his fellow officers. He was quickly revived and helped to a carriage. Another constable slipped and fell on the ice, badly bruising his leg. In all, it was a grisly scene to witness.

The frozen bodies were placed in the police carriage and transported to the morgue at the station hospital. Watson and I took our own carriage and returned to the hospital to await the autopsy results. The frozen bodies took several hours to defrost before they could be examined properly. We waited and kept warm with tea and hot soup, graciously supplied by the staff.

Finally, the word was given to start the autopsy. Inspectors Lestrade and Gregson, under the orders of Commissioner Charles Warren, took charge of the procedure.

"Dr. Watson, we could certainly use your help to conduct this investigation," said Commissioner Warren.

Dr. Watson stepped forward and set to work discovering the preliminary findings.

"First, the hanged man: the larynx has been crushed, indicating death by strangulation," he said definitively. "There are also some defensive wounds indicating that he put up a struggle, but to no avail. His hands and feet were bound before he was hanged."

Watson untied the hands and took thumb prints for identification. "Here, Lestrade, take these to the police files to check for possible identification."

The measurements of the entire body were taken for a more definitive check of the files.

Measurement of the length and breadth of the skull were noted, as well as the length of the foot size. Then, more delicate measurements were taken of the ear and index finger. These were taken to the police lab upstairs.

It took about three quarters of an hour to obtain results from the meager police files, for the practice of forensics was just beginning.

Meanwhile, close attention was paid to the body shape and size of the hanged man.

"A man of rather large, bulky body build, possibly a laborer, certainly not an office worker or bookkeeper. His hands were rough and calloused, used to hard work."

Soon Lestrade returned with the possible identification of the man.

"It appears that the man might have been David Blackwell, arrested for assault and disturbing the peace a few years ago. We just happen to have some of his records on file."

"David Blackwell! That would be Billy Blackwell's' brother!" I said. "But why would Billy Blackwell kill his own brother?"

"Falling out among thieves!" ventured Watson.

"But to kill your own brother!" exclaimed Lestrade.

"It would be expected of someone who would abandon a drowning boy, years ago," I said angrily.

"But how did Billy fall into the icy pond?" asked Watson.

"I surmise he must have slipped when he hung his brother from the icy branch. And no one had been around to help him when he fell. Billy had a black heart that suffered no opposition to his will. His brother and he must have quarreled over some important dispute and Billy took revenge. David's disobedience had deadly consequences," I explained.

"And Billy shared those consequences ... a case of poetic justice, I would say," exclaimed Watson.

The burial service was brief, for a prisoner interment was considered a disgrace to society. Watson and I watched as the convicts' bodies were lowered into shallow graves, and dirt shoveled over them. No words were spoken on their behalf!

Of the few mourners gathered around the grave sites, I thought I recognized someone off in the distance. Her red hair was showing through a dark veil, which covered most of her face. Could this be Barbara, the girl who had so cruelly mocked the struggling Matthew, "I'm not getting wet to help that silly boy!"?

I began to make my way toward her, but when she saw me, she began to run away. Then, slipping on the icy path, she fell and hurt her ankle. Lying helpless, she awaited our inevitable meeting.

"Barbara, is that you?" I said, trying to help her.

"Yes, Mr. Sherlock Holmes, it's Barbara. I've followed your exploits ever since that day on the ice, so long ago."

She got to her feet and leaning on me for support, she said angrily, "So the great Sherlock Holmes has finally caught up with me!"

In her struggle to get up, her black veil fell to the ground, revealing a horrible sight.

"Your face!" I said. "What has happened to you?"

"A legacy of my association with that devil, Billy Blackwell, that vicious beast!"

Her face was hideously scarred and disfigured. Cut marks crossed her cheeks and acid burn marks covered her forehead and eyes.

"Did Billy do this?" I asked, not believing what I saw.

"Who else? Only that evil monster could think of such a punishment. And after my loyalty and devotion to him for all these years!"

"What do you mean punishment?" I asked.

"Billy caught his brother, David, and I together in an innocent meeting, and flew into a rage. Before we could explain, he extracted his revenge. He said he'd fix me so no other man would look at me again ... and you saw what he did to David!

"When he was through strangling David, he strung him up on the highest branch. But, in getting his revenge, he lost his balance and fell into the icy water below. After what he did to me, I enjoyed watching him thrash about, screaming at the top of his voice for help. I just stood there laughing."

Watson spoke up.

"This woman is a murderess! She is involved with the death of your childhood friend and certainly let another man die without any effort to save him. She should go to prison for her part in the affairs."

"No, Watson, she is condemned to a prison much worse ... a life sentence of loneliness and despair," I said in judgment.

"But, Holmes!" protested Watson, "the law ... "

"Justice has been done, Watson, far more effectively than any law. Divine justice has interceded where no mortal justice could prevail. We must let her go to live out her life sentence alone," I declared.

Watson and I returned to our home at 221B Baker Street later that day. After an early supper, courtesy of Mrs. Hudson, we all sat around the crackling fireplace, each enjoying a glass of port wine. I took to my pipe and a good smoke.

"You need some time to heal your mind and body," advised Mrs. Hudson. "It's been a long and trying day."

I sensed an air of motherly concern in her voice, for she was possessed of a woman's intuition and kindness that showed itself when the occasion required it.

There were a few moments of tranquility; then Watson spoke.

"One wonders at the circumstances that warp and bend a person's life to evil!"

"There, but for the grace of God ..." replied Mrs. Hudson.

"There, but for the grace of good friends and family ..." I stated. "For that is the only protection against tragedy, violence, and injustice. And with your help, my dear friends, perhaps the painful memory of my best friend's tragic death can now be laid to rest."

I glanced at the carved statue of the wooden horse, on the fireplace mantle, and then I took a few more puffs on my pipe and watched the smoke rise in twisted tangles, vanishing in the air.

ADVENTURE No. 5

The da Vinci Madonna

*This case proved to be
one of my most embarrassing experiences!*

THE DA VINCI MADONNA

I t was one of those lazy, uneventful Sunday afternoons, when Watson and I were relaxing in our favorite chairs beside the fireplace. Glancing over the weeks' news events, we shared sections of the London Times with each other.

"Ah, me!" I sighed, expressing my boredom with the uneventfulness of the last few months' happenings.

"What's the matter, Holmes?" inquired Watson, fully aware of the problem.

"It seems as if crime has taken a holiday and left me no opportunities to exercise my restless brain!" I replied, feeling totally frustrated.

"I hope this boredom will not encourage you to revert to that seven per cent solution," said Watson, fearing a return to my dreadful habit.

"I've been thinking of it," I offhandedly responded.

"Good heavens, Holmes! Not that again," warned Watson. "I fear for your life, my good friend!" he continued, thoroughly upset.

Ignoring his brotherly concern for me, I just drifted into deep thought, settling into my comfortable chair.

After what seemed like only a moment later, fate seemed to knock at the door in the person of Mrs. Hudson. Her disturbing knock and frenzied voice jarred us from our complacency.

"Mr. Holmes. Dr. Watson. I need your help!"

Rushing to open the door, we found Mrs. Hudson desperately attempting to support a stranger who seemed to be hurt. The poor woman could hardly bear the weight of his slumped body.

"Watson, you help the man over to the sofa and I'll take the large package he is carrying."

The stranger dropped onto the couch and muttered the words, "da Vinci Madonna, the Black Madonna … worth a fortune!"

With that, the poor man gasped his last breath and died.

"Too late to help him," said Watson, helplessly.

Mrs. Hudson began to cry hysterically.

"The poor man just appeared at the front door with a package for you, Mr. Holmes. I didn't know just what to do!"

"You did just fine, Mrs. Hudson. He was beyond all help. You couldn't have done anything more for him."

Watson made some tea to calm her nerves and settled her into a chair.

"Shouldn't we summon the police, Holmes?"

"Maybe we should, but first let's see what's in the package."

The mysterious object lay on the chesterfield lounge chair, where it had been dropped.

"Now, to the mysterious package!"

Hastily, we tore off the wrappings of the carefully wrapped package. It took some time as it was covered with many layers to protect the contents.

"Finally!" I said, hardly able to hold back my excitement. "The last wrapping is undone!"

"What is it?" asked Watson, trembling with anticipation.

There, before us, stood an exquisitely carved head and shoulder statue of a beautiful woman, set in a contemplative pose. Curiously it was carved in black marble … a Black Madonna.

I recognized it immediately!

"It's the black marble statue of the virgin Madonna," I exclaimed in astonishment.

"Holmes, what does this mean? Who?" stammered Watson. But before he could say anything further, I interrupted.

"I believe it is the fabled Black Madonna that is rumored to have been carved by the young Leonardo da Vinci!"

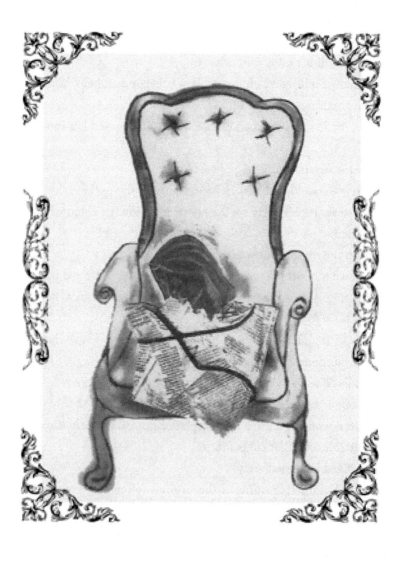

"But I thought da Vinci was a painter, not a sculptor," said Watson, somewhat confused.

"And probably the world's greatest painter," I explained. "But when the young Leonardo was first enrolled at the great art studio of André Verrocchio, there was some controversy as to which field of study he would undertake … painting or sculpture. He was a very talented lad and could do just about anything!"

"Amazing!" said Watson.

"How did he come to choose painting?" asked Mrs. Hudson, now recovered from her initial shock.

"Well, it seemed the Master Verrocchio decided that Leonardo should choose the direction of his life for himself. At that time, in Renaissance Italy, all the rage was concerned with the properties of light. The greatest painters were experimenting with capturing the effects of light on objects. Da Vinci applied his efforts to painting on canvas, leaving behind the study of sculpture."

"What about the Black Madonna?" asked Mrs. Hudson.

"Well, according to da Vinci scholars, Leonardo carved the statue as an entrance requirement for the academy. Marvelous as it was, his painting ability excelled even his sculptural talents. Or at least, that is the story that has come down through historical fable!"

"Then this could be that famed Black Madonna sculpture of Leonardo da Vinci!" exclaimed Watson.

"Yes, and as such, it is priceless, both to collectors and historians," I remarked.

"And if it is that valuable, then the criminal element in society will definitely be after it!" warned Watson.

"That is exactly my fear," I agreed. "We must first get Inspector Lestrade involved with the affair and also see to the statue's safekeeping."

Then Mrs. Hudson spoke up. "I should tell you, Mr. Holmes, that when the stranger first came to the door, he warned me that he had been followed. The man who attacked him knew he had reached us and probably guessed that the package might end up in your hands. So, be very careful!"

"Thank you for that information. I shall be ever vigilant," I replied.

Inspector Lestrade was called and he informed us that he would be about fifteen to twenty minutes before he could get here.

"Well, we have to wait for the inspector to arrive and take care of the body," I said. "I suggest that the wisest course would be to keep the knowledge of the Black Madonna a secret until we find out more about its origins."

"Perhaps we can eventually transport it to the National Gallery, where it can be securely housed and properly presented to the public in a gala display," suggested Watson.

"Good idea, Watson!" I agreed. "Meanwhile, let's place the statue in the secret crypt behind the fireplace. It will be safe there!" I suggested.

The statue was sequestered behind the fireplace and we waited for Inspector Lestrade to arrive.

While we were waiting, Mrs. Hudson was curious about Leonardo da Vinci.

"It seems, Mr. Holmes, that Leonardo gave up the possibility of a great sculpture career," she said.

"Well, as I said, Mrs. Hudson, he was fascinated with concepts of light. He had a unique ability to understand extreme opposites and to explore the unknown. He could feel comfortable with uncertainty or 'foggy thinking'. In time he became an expert at the sfumato technique of painting."

"Sfumato? What is that?" questioned Mrs. Hudson.

"Sfumato can be viewed as a willingness to engage in uncertainties, ambiguities, and juxtaposition of non-harmonious constructs!" I explained.

"What do you mean by non-harmonious constructs?" said Mrs. Hudson, thoroughly confused.

"Well, Leonardo's experiments with man-in-flight are a direct contradiction to the terrestrial nature of humans. Also, using machines for mechanical advantage is contrary to the feeble strength of man against nature!"

"But what has this to do with sfumato?" asked Mrs. Hudson, even more confused. "It all sounds too complicated to me!"

"Let me try to explain it with a simple example." I said. "Suppose you draw a figure with a pencil. You will produce a sharp and definite outline of that figure."

"Of course, Mr. Holmes, everyone knows that!"

"Well then, if you smudge the pencil marks with your finger, you will end up with a blurry, non-distinct, smoky outline … sfumato! That's what the Italians call 'vanishing like smoke'! No harsh outlines."

"Oh! It's not too hard to understand, after all! Thank you, Mr. Holmes, for explaining it in the King's English! And so, the blurring of an object makes it look more mysterious and ambiguous, and yet real!" she replied, feeling more comfortable with the idea.

"Exactly! Now you have it!" I replied, greatly satisfied that I had conveyed the idea to her. "And in life you actually don't see things with a dark and definite background. Rather, they fade gently and subtly into the background … sfumato! That is the secret of the Mona Lisa painting … his greatest achievement."

"Yes, yes, elementary … sfumato … Mona Lisa!" commented Watson, who has been silently listening.

"Right you are, Watson," I replied, suppressing a smile.

Then, an interrupting knock at the door saved us all from the tedious session. It was Lestrade. He inspected the body, and after a brief conversation concerning the particulars of that afternoon, he and his colleagues removed the body.

Watson and I were now alone, having settled Mrs. Hudson back down to her apartment. Trying to regain the peace and calmness of the earlier afternoon, we set to relaxing with the London Times again. But persistent fate stepped in again in the form of a mysterious letter that was delivered late that evening. It stated:

"If you wish to discover the true story of the Black Madonna, come to the Psychic House of Future's End in White Chapel at eight o'clock tonight. All will be told to you. Knock twice and wait to be admitted!"

"We must be careful," warned Watson. "It might be a trap or attempt to get the statue."

"Yes," I agreed. "It's best to keep our special lady hidden behind the fireplace."

As time for our departure drew near, we planned our journey into the darkness and danger of White Chapel.

"Let's not take the first cab, Watson. I fear it might hold peril for us. Then, the second cab will be just as good!"

Sure enough, the first cab hailed was driven by a rough-mannered driver, and so we passed it by. The second cab seemed more suited to our needs, and so Watson and I got in.

As we traveled down to White Chapel, we both sat silently awaiting our fate. When we reached the dark and winding streets of the district, we cautiously searched for the meeting place where we were to get our information. We found the old building labeled 'The Psychic House of Future's End'. We paid the cabbie, who then quickly exited the area.

We knocked twice and waited. We were greeted by a mysterious woman in black. Her face was hidden behind a black veil. Only the shadowy outline of her face was visible.

"Come in. I am Nalla, your psychic reader. I will read the past, present, and future of your lives for you."

"We have come for information about the Black Madonna," I said to the lady Nalla.

"Yes," she replied. As she moved about, the veil shifted, slightly revealing only vague features of her face. Her voice was rough, more like a man than a woman.

"Your mysterious statue has come on the Italian cargo ship 'Bona Fortuna'. It sailed a few weeks ago from Licata, a seaport on the coast of Sicily. The captain, Christopher Zarbo, was charged with delivering it to a certain collector in London. However, it seems he did not complete his assignment. That is all I can tell you at this time."

"What is our role in the care of this package?" I asked.

She avoided a direct answer.

"Sherlock Holmes," she said, "I see your future very clearly. Behold this Prophecy of Doom:

"The Sands of Time slip through our fingers

This Prophecy of Doom in my sight lingers

Let him who laughs and turns away

Lament his fate some future day."

She went on further:

"Beware the Shadows of the Night

'Round the bend and out of sight

A vision of your death I see

A final ending waits for thee!"

"Sherlock Holmes, you will meet three twisted and gruesome challenges of death. They will be unlike any others you have previously encountered. Each challenge will require your greatest efforts to survive.

"The first challenge is a test of strength.

"The second challenge will take all your cunning.

"The third challenge will need luck to survive.

"If you are not up to these challenges, your life will be a short one. Now go, I can tell you no more!"

With that, the mysterious lady disappeared out a back door. There was nothing left to do but return home. As we left the building, we walked through the dark, deserted streets, hoping to hail a cab. But cabs did not frequent this gloomy section of town. The further we walked the more desolate was our predicament. Then, all at once, three thugs stepped up behind us.

"Watson, look out!" I shouted.

A man with a large knife came up to Watson. But Watson acted quickly, clutching the evil man's throat with one hand and wrestling with the knife hand with his other. Watson's strangle hold on the thug effectively rendered him unconscious.

I treated the second thug to a left jab and then a right hook to the jaw. He went down quickly and lay there dazed.

The third man was a different problem. He was huge and muscular. In his right hand he held a large club, which he swung at me. I ducked and pulled his arm to set him off balance. He fell hard on the ground hitting his head and rendered himself unconscious. We had passed our test of strength, the first challenge.

But now it was time to exit the neighborhood. We ran out of the area as fast as we could and finally reached a waiting cab. We jumped in and headed for home.

The topic of conversation all the way home was the prediction of the lady Nalla concerning my imminent death. Watson was very concerned about the threat to our lives, but I just laughed it off.

"We've passed the first test of the three challenges and, I trust, we will pass the others," I said, taking the whole matter lightly.

When we arrived home at Baker Street, I was chiding Watson for his foolish beliefs in 'parlor tricks'. But as we entered the apartment, it soon became evident that Watson's fears were well-founded!

The whole room was in an uproar … papers and books thrown all around.

"Holmes, we have been burglarized!"

I quickly checked the secret hiding place behind the fireplace.

"Yes, Watson, but it seems that they have not found what they were looking for. The Black Madonna is still safely hidden behind the fireplace. We seem to have a charmed life, my friend. We have met the second challenge … that of cunning. The statue is safe due to our precaution of hiding it. I had a premonition that the trip to the lady Nalla was a trick to get us out of the flat so that thieves could pay us a visit. But we out-smarted them."

Watson threw up his hands and gasped.

"Holmes, this puzzle is all mixed up! Everything is out of order! Even the psychic Nalla is not in the natural order of things!"

I suddenly had a flash of inspiration.

"Not in the natural order … an anagram!"

"A what?" blurted the puzzled Watson.

I wrote the name 'Nalla' down on a piece of paper. Then I transposed the letters, rearranging them in a reverse order.

"Holmes, for heaven's sake, what are you doodling?" asked Watson.

"An anagram!" I repeated. "Of course! I knew something was odd about the lady Nalla … her rough voice, her dark veil. It was all a disguise!"

"A disguise?" said Watson thoroughly confused.

"Yes, if you transpose the letters of 'Nalla', you get 'Allan', and you discover the hidden identity of our psychic. Allan is a female impersonator! A cross dresser! No wonder he knew what would happen to us on the way home … he planned it!"

"But who is Allan?" asked Watson.

"That is what we must discover! We will start out early tomorrow to seek out this diabolical villain. First, we must get a good night's rest."

We set out early the next morning with the precious statue in our procession. We had finally determined that it should be delivered to the National Gallery, where it could be displayed to the public in proper fashion. The foggy London morning sky seemed like a homage to a Leonardo sfumato painting … a masterful blend of light and shadow that lent a magical, dream-like fantasy to the experience.

The streets were becoming more congested now, as the cabs carrying the upper-class citizens of London to their destinations pushed on. Occasional minor collisions of the cabs prompted some of the cabbies to challenge their fellows' driving skills, and a number of arguments broke out as the labyrinth of traffic slowly moved on.

As we drove down the street, we noticed that another cab seemed to be coming up too closely, as if to ram us! Sure enough, the approaching cab speeded up as its driver yelled, "I, Allan, nephew of James Moriarty, bring death to the great Sherlock Holmes!"

The next second, we were rammed broadside! Our cab skidded and began to overturn.

"Jump Watson! Get clear of the cab!" I yelled.

I was thrown headlong onto the side of the road. I held the precious statue in my hands, but the force of the landing loosened it and it flew a few feet away. Fortunately, it landed on soft, grassy ground and was not damaged. I was not so lucky. Using my hands to cushion my fall, I sprained my right wrist.

"Ow!" I cried out. "My hand!"

Watson, having landed on his feet, ran over to me.

"Holmes, are you alright?"

"Don't worry about me, get the statue!" I cried.

But it was too late. The villainous Allan had sprung from his cab and grabbed the statue, exclaiming "Too bad, Mr. Holmes. It looks like you failed on the third challenge. Your luck has run out! My uncle, James, will be proud of me!"

With that he jumped into his cab, which had escaped any major damage and sped away down Tower Bridge Street.

I lay there stunned for a moment, my right hand throbbing in pain. The overcrowded street was now in turmoil, a chaos of cabs and horses in complete disarray. By this time the police force had arrived, with Lestrade in command.

"Holmes," he said, coming to my aid. "You could have been killed!"

"Quick, Lestrade, we must engage another cab and be off after him!"

"Be off after who? I don't understand!"

"I'll explain as we ride," I answered.

So, Watson, Lestrade, and I got into another cab and made our way at top speed down the street after the villainous Allan Moriarty. As we proceeded at break neck speed trying to catch up with our culprit, I explained the fascinating story of the da Vinci Madonna to Lestrade.

I bitterly mumbled, "Allan Moriarty, another drop of poison in the already blemished bloodline of the Moriartys!"

Lestrade agreed. "Is there no end to the twisted personalities of that family?"

In a few minutes we passed the Tower of London, and finally arrived at Tower Bridge. A large crowd had assembled to view the lone figure standing at the top of one of the towers. It was Allan! He had climbed to the top of Tower Bridge and was waving the Madonna statue frantically. He shouted something, but his voice could not be heard in the street below.

"Holmes! What shall we do?" exclaimed Watson.

"There is only one thing to do!" I replied, firmly.

"No, Holmes. You can't!" warned Lestrade.

"I must climb the tower and save the statue and Allan, if I can!" I insisted.

Before they could stop me, I was on my way up to the tower. The pain in my wrist was as intense as ever, but I continued to climb. As I approached the top, I could hear Allan's ravings.

"Holmes, you'll never see this again! My uncle will possess it or no one will!"

"Allan, stop this nonsense and give up the fight!"

"Never!" he screamed.

Just as I was about to reach him, he jumped away and slipped. Now he was hanging on for his life to a cross rail of the tower. I reached down just in time to catch his hand, preventing him from falling to a horrible death!

Now, letting go of the statue, he pleaded with me, "Help me, Mr. Holmes. Help me!"

I watched the statue tumble down into the muddy Thames River, never to be seen again.

Allan held on desperately to my arm and I to his, but then as his grip loosened on my right arm, I could no longer stand the pain.

"I can't hold on any longer!" Slowly and painfully my hand lost its grip on the panicking young figure, slipping further and further from my grasp.

"Help, Mr. Holmes! Don't let me fall ... please!"

But it was no use. I let go!

The poor young man let out a terrible scream as he plunged down into the treacherous waters of the Thames.

"I'm sorry! I'm sorry!" I cried out.

Then, from the distance I heard, "Holmes! Holmes!"

A voice was calling out to me from far, far away.

"Holmes, you're dreaming. Wake up, for heaven's sake!"

It was Watson, shaking me from my dream.

"Watson!" I said, awakening from my terrible nightmare. My brain was still foggy, as if refusing to come back to the events of the real world. My dream was so vivid and horrifying, that I had trouble shaking it.

"You were dreaming, Holmes. Everything is all right," said Watson, in an attempt to calm me down.

My first words were: "There is no da Vinci Madonna? … no nephew of Moriarty?"

"What are you talking about, my dear fellow?" answered Watson, concerned for my sanity.

I tried to explain.

"I thought that we received a mysterious package … the Black Madonna, created by Leonardo da Vinci and that Moriarty's nephew, Allan, had stolen it and tried to escape by climbing to the top of Tower Bridge!"

"No, no, Holmes. It was all in your imagination!"

"But it seemed so real, Watson," I insisted.

"The more real the nightmare, the more deeply in the mind it is buried," responded Watson. "Moriarty is embedded in your psyche!"

"What happened?" I said, bewildered.

"You fell into a deep sleep in your chair and your slumber turned into a raging nightmare."

"Thank heaven," I sighed. "Can you image a second generation of the Moriarty family? It's too dreadful to think of!"

"We have enough trouble with the original!" laughed Watson.

"So, we have. So, we have," I replied, thankful that the world had to contend with only one. "And as to the legendary Black Madonna, Leonardo was a man of legends ... one more or less will not diminish his fame."

I mused: "Da Vinci Madonna ... how marvelously inventive the human mind."

Watson laughed, "Holmes, I think you need a vacation!"

I laughed, "Rightly so, Watson. Rightly so."

ADVENTURE NO. 6
The Case of the
Amazing Invisible Man

THE CASE OF THE AMAZING INVISIBLE MAN

Little did I know that I was about to be entangled in one of the most bizarre and dangerous cases of my entire career. What started out as a normal day, turned into an adventure that almost ended in my death!

I was returning from one of my infrequent visits to the office of my older brother, Mycroft, at the Diogenes Club, having consulted with him on a particularly involved government matter. Although he possessed a brilliant mind for these matters, he occasionally considered seeking my help with certain bizarre cases, although begrudgingly. I would have called it "The Assessor's Assassin" had circumstances not pulled me in another direction.

I must say, I was particularly satisfied with my older brother's need to acknowledge my talents in the field of crime solving. It might be said that a certain degree of brotherly rivalry existed between the two of us. Unfortunately, that is often the situation between family members born too closely together. How unlike the strong bond of friendship that existed between my roommate, Dr. Watson, and me. Watson was as true in friendship as my older brother was irritating in his condescension toward me. But that is often the nature of friends and family; for friends are chosen for compatibility, whereas family occurs by inevitability.

Oh well, be that as it may, my thoughts were rudely diverted from my contemplation by the piercing calls of a young newsboy. "Extra! Extra! Read all about it! The greatest crime of the century."

"Here, lad. I'll take a copy!"

"Yes, Sir, one copper please," was his reply.

I greedily scanned the front-page article like a hungry lion at his meal.

"The crime of the century ... the centerpiece of the Crown Jewels has been stolen. The spectacular replacement crown of Edward the Confessor has vanished into thin air without a trace!"

I read further, searching for details.

Guards at the Tower of London say they have no clue as to the method of theft. One moment the crown was there, the next it was gone!

The Royal Family has issued a statement. "This is a dark day in the history of England! There is a sizable reward for its recovery."

The article went on to fill in the history of the crown.

The replacement crown was made in 1660, after the original crown of St. Edward was destroyed during the English Civil War in 1649. St. Edward's Crown has been used in all succeeding coronation ceremonies of the sovereigns of England since then.

"Humbug," I muttered. "This article is disappointingly scarce in the important details of the theft. All it says is that the jewels have mysteriously vanished into thin air! Preposterous! Thin air!"

The article concluded with the obvious.

"The iconic crown is a symbolic bridge from past to present and marks the passage of power from one ruler to the next. It is the defining element of English kingship."

By now I had reached the door at Baker Street and, flinging it open, I hurried upstairs to the apartment that I shared with Dr. Watson. I took two stairs at a time, not wanting to waste a moment.

"Watson, did you hear?" I said as I burst through the door of our flat. "The Crown Jewels ..."

"Yes, Holmes, I heard the newsboy calling out on the street below," answered Watson. "Holmes, what is this world coming to?"

"Yes, Watson, criminals are getting more bold! They have no respect for the very foundations of our civilization ... nothing is sacred anymore!"

Watson hesitated and then replied, "I hope this doesn't spoil our plans for my birthday celebration ... it's August 7th, you know!"

"Oh no, Watson, our plans for dinner and theatre are firmly made for the Egyptian Hall Theatre, tonight!"

We had chosen the Egyptian Hall Theatre for our night out because it was a showcase for unusual acts of human existence … so-called "freak shows."

Now showing were acts such as the "Siamese Twins, conjoined brothers, Chang and Eng Brinker", and the American Dwarf, Charles Sherwood Stratton, also known as "General Tom Thumb." At the other end of the scale, was "Chang, the Chinese Giant," who was over eight feet tall!

Altogether, the Egyptian Hall Theatre has the reputation of being England's House of Mystery.

For a limited engagement, the celebrated magician, Primo Manzella, would be appearing. He was a new act, just arrived from Budapest.

As we approached the Hall in our Hansom Cab, the grand façade, done in Egyptian style, came into view. It stood out from the Georgian architecture surrounding it. Many of its details were copied from the Dendera Temple in Egypt. Above the entrance were two large stone figures of Isis and Osiris. Inside was a Grand Hall, in which other Egyptian features were displayed.

We took out seats at a table near the stage. Dinner was served and our waiter opened a bottle of champagne, pouring a full glass for each of us.

"Here's to you, Watson," I said as I toasted my good friend.

"To the truest friend a man every had!" I continued.

We lifted our glasses and they come together with a tinkling sound of finest crystal.

"Thank you, Holmes. The feeling is mutual!"

We were both looking forward to the evening's performance and there was an air of excitement throughout the room.

Then, one by one, the entertainment began and the human oddities were paraded on stage.

The advance notice for the feature performance stated that the Great Primo Manzella would display an "act of invisibility." It was rumored that he had somehow mastered the secret technique of invisibility!

"I don't believe it!" said Watson as he sipped his glass of champagne.

I was more cautious. "I'll reserve judgment," I said, "until I see his act!"

All at once the lights in the room went down and as we sat in darkness, the curtain opened to a brightly lit stage.

A booming voice rang out. "Ladies and gentlemen, the act you've all been waiting for ... the Great Primo Manzella."

We all applauded the empty stage!

Then, to our amazement, a small table seemed to rise and float through the air. It settled down in the middle of the stage.

Then, just as amazingly, a chair followed, and set right down next to the table!

Then a voice, with a foreign accent, called out!

"Good evening, ladies and gentlemen. Welcome to this evening's performance."

To everyone's astonishment, a man stepped out of what seemed to be an invisible coat and bowed to the audience.

It was true! The Great Manzella had found the secret of invisibility!

I turned to Watson. "What do you say now, my skeptical friend?"

"If I hadn't seen it with my own eyes, I would not have believed it!" he replied somewhat embarrassed and astounded.

The rest of the performance that night consisted of various versions of invisibility tricks.

In the final phase of his act, he passed among the members of the audience, invisible, and took various items off the table without the audience knowing it.

He was so quick that no one could catch sight of his hand. As he passed our table he whispered, "Hope you enjoyed the performance, Mr. Holmes!"

The performance ended with his total disappearance, which gained him an overwhelming round of applause from the audience.

All the way home, Watson and I were absorbed in the excitement of the evening's performance.

"How did he know my identity, Watson?" It was a mystery!

We arrived at home quite late and Watson attempted to consult his pocket watch.

"Heavens, Holmes, my watch is gone!"

"What do you mean, Watson?"

"It must have been taken during the performance!"

"No doubt when the Great Manzella came to the table!" I guessed.

"It was given to me for distinguished service when I left the army. It has great value, Holmes."

"Well, Watson, there's nothing we can do about it now. Tomorrow is another day!"

Watson headed to bed, weary and disappointed.

But I decided to stay up and explore an idea that I had read in an obscure magazine about optics. The article described a little-known phenomenon that resulted from the placement of two mirrors in a specific angle to each other, such that the light between them would be invisible to the naked eye. I wondered, could a series of small mirrors, attached together in that precise way cause invisibility over a large area? Then, one could construct an "invisibility coat" which, when worn, would cause a person to appear invisible!

While Watson slept, I took a large mirror from the hallway and carefully cut it into small pieces with a cutting tool from my kit. I experimented with positioning each piece in just the right way on an old coat of mine.

I worked feverously and pursued my experiment. Soon, every available mirror in the house had fallen victim to my obsession!

I worked all night, and by morning, "Eureka!" I had my "invisibility coat!"

The morning sun had lit up the parlor and, exhausted from the night's indulgence, I decided to sit in my favorite chesterfield lounge chair by the fireplace. I reached for my pipe and, still wearing my "invisibility coat," I took a few puffs.

Watson had just gotten up from bed and, walking into the parlor, saw a disembodied pipe sending smoke puffs into the air.

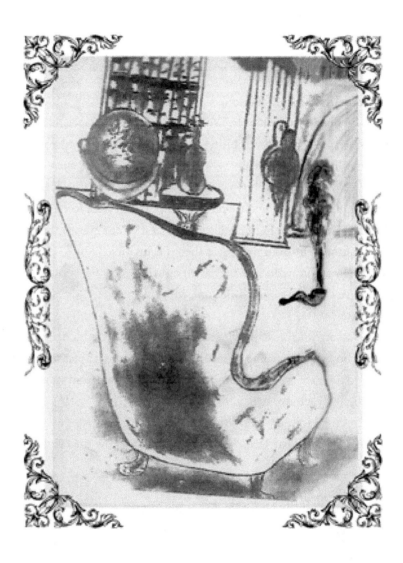

"What in the name of heaven!" he cried.

I gave one more puff of smoke into the air. Then I announced myself.

"Good morning, Watson."

The poor man almost fainted.

"Holmes, it that you?"

"Yes, Watson. I've solved the mystery of invisibility! It's all done with mirrors!"

"Mirrors?" questioned Watson.

"Yes," I replied, triumphantly. "When placed in the proper relationship to each other, we achieve invisibility! I have made a coat of mirrors that confers invisibility to the wearer.

"You see, Watson, invisibility is playing with light, so that it does not reach the intended object and therefore cannot reflect back to our eyes. We see the object only if the light is reflected off of it to our eyes. If there is no reflection of the light from the object then it is invisible to us."

"But Holmes, how can you 'play' with light?"

"As I have said, Watson, it's all done with mirrors!"

"Mirrors?"

"Yes, Watson, mirrors can reflect light away from its intended target object. So we just arrange an assemblage of mirrors at just the right angles as to distract the light from its intended course ... that is, we 'play' with the light to achieve invisibility!"

"Astounding, Holmes," said Watson in disbelief.

"Elementary, my dear Watson. And now I know how the crime of the century was committed!"

"You do?" asked, Watson, intrigued.

"Remember that the papers said that the Crown Jewels disappeared without a trace?"

"Yes, Holmes. But what does that tell us?"

"Without a trace!" I repeated. "Who do we know that is able to vanish without a trace, my dear fellow?"

"Why the Great Primo Manzella!" replied Watson.

"Yes, and we must visit him before he has a chance to break up the jewels and dispose of them!" I answered. "And maybe we can also retrieve your watch!"

"Where can we look for him?" asked Watson, eagerly.

"Where else but his back stage room at the Egyptian Hall Theatre. I'm sure he is using it as his headquarters."

So, we hopped into a cab and sped to the theatre. I brought my invisibility coat with me, just in case it should be needed.

"Why the coat?" asked Watson.

"To even the odds," I remarked. "The game's a foot, Watson!"

When we arrived at the theatre, everything was dark.

"Let's go into the stage entrance, Watson."

Lucky for us, the door was left open.

We made our way through the dark backstage corridor. In the distance I saw a faint light coming in from a slightly open door.

"Our quarry is just ahead, Watson," I whispered.

We came upon the Great Primo just as he was admiring his prize crown in the mirror.

"It's all mine!" he said, admiring the crown.

"A little premature, my twisted fellow!" I snarled.

He reacted with lightning reflexes, grabbing his invisibility coat. He ran across the stage and, putting on his coat, began to climb the narrow stairs to the gangway above. All we could hear was a faint clinking of Watson's watch against the glass mirrors.

"Holmes, he has disappeared," cried Watson.

"And so shall I," I said putting on my invisibility coat.

I used the clinking of Watson's watch against the glass mirrors to follow Primo's progress along the catwalk above the stage area. With each step I took, I was aware that one false step could lead to my death if I slipped off the narrow pathway before me. Primo's progress was faster and surer than mine, for he had become accustomed to moving about while invisible. Primo was clever! Every once in a while, he would stand perfectly still and I was at a loss as to his whereabouts.

Once, he lay back, waiting for me, and with a great push, almost sent me to my death, crashing to the stage floor below. It was all I could do to hang on to a railing to keep from falling.

"Mr. Holmes, you'll never catch me. I am used to walking about in my invisibility coat … you are not."

"Don't overestimate your ability, Primo. I'm learning fast!"

With one hand gripping a railing, I reached out to where I judged him to be standing. But I missed and almost let go of my grasp!

"Ha! Ha! Mr. Holmes. It's not so easy as you think!" taunted Primo.

He was right, but I couldn't admit it to him.

"You won't get away, my evil friend!"

"Maybe this time you've bit off more than you can chew, Mr. Detective!"

"Don't you believe it!" I countered.

"Come and get me, Mr. Holmes!" he taunted.

Then, all at once, Watson's watch came to the rescue. Primo had carelessly attached it to his belt. The watch came loose and fell, clanking at his feet. I immediately lunged at him, and as he stepped aside to dodge my advance, his foot slipped and, with a hideous scream, plunged down to the stage floor below! His fall was accompanied with the deafening crash of hundreds of pieces of glass as the invisibility coat was smashed beyond all use.

"Holmes, are you alright?" cried Watson.

"Yes, Watson, Primo has met his doom!"

I carefully eased my way down from the catwalk and stairway to the stage below.

There, on the stage floor, was the half visible, half invisible body of the Great Primo.

"Holmes, the villain has met his end, and St. Edward's Crown recovered. Good work!" congratulated Watson.

"Oh, by the way, Watson, here is your watch!"

"Holmes, you recovered it for me. It has great sentimental value for me."

"It had greater practical value for me, Watson. When it fell out of Primo's pocket on the catwalk, it revealed his position and afforded me the opportunity to flip him off balance. He lost his footing and fell to his death!"

"I shudder to think what would have happened if he hadn't stolen my watch, Holmes!"

"Yes, Watson, whether the Crown Jewels or a simple pocket watch, the Great Primo could not resist the basic impulse to acquire by theft. That was his downfall! It is curious that even the most inconsequential act can alter the delicate balance of fate! It was fortunate for me that his baser acquisitive instinct guided his behavior."

"What next, Holmes?"

"We shall return the Crown without having to explain the details of invisibility."

"How can we do that?" questioned Watson.

"We will return the jewels the same way they were taken … with the invisibility coat!"

"What about Primo?" asked Watson.

"Primo will be buried in an unmarked grave. No crime was committed, since I acted in self-defense!"

That night, I dressed in my invisibility coat, secretly passed the guards on duty and carefully replaced the crown to its rightful place.

The result in the newspapers the next day was spectacular!

"Look here, Holmes," said Watson, pointing to the headlines. "The headlines report that the Crown Jewels have reappeared just as mysteriously as they had vanished. The Royal Family reports that they are 'pleased and confident that the Tradition of the Monarchy is safe once again'!"

"Yes, Watson. All is right with the world! And now for the final act of this bizarre case."

"And what is that, Holmes?"

I took a hammer out of my tool kit.

Smash! Smash! Smash!

The "invisibility coat" was no more ... now only a pile of glass fragments.

"Holmes, what are you doing?"

"The secret of invisibility must not be revealed to the public."

"Why not, Holmes. It's a great power for mankind," insisted Watson.

"Yes, too great a power to let loose in our time, when criminals are all around us! This power must be reserved for a future time, when men can trust each other in a more brotherly fashion."

"Is such a time possible, Holmes?"

"We can only hope, Watson, we can only hope!"

"But, Holmes, no one will ever know how you saved St. Edward's Crown."

"Yes, Watson, and no one will ever know of the invisibility coat. An invention before its time can be a threat rather than a boon to society. Sometimes it must wait to fit into the natural order of a society's development to be of value."

"Yes, Holmes, but it's a shame to lose such a wonder!"

I stuffed the fragments of the invisibility coat into an old barrel. Only the crumbled fragments of glass bore witness to the fabulous coat. The tiny pieces reflected the gas light in the room and shone like stars on a clear summer night.

"Stars in a bucket, Watson. Stars in a bucket!"